'Den...re going to be my woman, Rayne. You *are* my woman. Understand?' he breathed against the sensitised hollow of her ear. 'Otherwise why would you let me do this?'

His fingers found her breast, making her gasp.

'Or...'

His ... hand slid down her body, caressing, its ...ng through her clothes.

...ingsley demanded huskily. 'If you can't ...t, too?'

...ed to protest. She knew she should. ...could she, she demanded chaotically of ...when she knew that she had been made ...That she was his and always had been, ...even if her mind recognised the treachery ...wledging it her body wouldn't listen.

But... ad to make it listen…

He's ... enemy. So what does that make you?

Elizabeth Power wanted to be a writer from a very early age, but it wasn't until she was nearly thirty that she took to writing seriously. Writing is now her life. Travelling ranks very highly among her pleasures, and so many places she has visited have been recreated in her books. Living in England's West Country, Elizabeth likes nothing better than taking walks with her husband along the coast or in the adjoining woods, and enjoying all the wonders that nature has to offer.

Recent titles by the same author:

BACK IN THE LION'S DEN
SINS OF THE PAST
FOR REVENGE OR REDEMPTION

Did you know these are also available as eBoo
Visit www.millsandboon.co.uk

A DELICIOUS
DECEPTION

BY
ELIZABETH POWER

First published in Great Britain 2012
by Mills & Boon, an imprint of Harlequin (UK) Limited.
Harlequin (UK) Limited, Eton House, 18-24 Paradise Road,
Richmond, Surrey TW9 1SR

© Elizabeth Power 2012

ISBN: 978 0 263 89118 8

Harlequin (UK) policy is to use papers that are natural, renewable and recyclable products and made from wood grown in sustainable forests. The logging and manufacturing process conform to the legal environmental regulations of the country of origin.

Printed and bound in Spain
by Blackprint CPI, Barcelona

A DELICIOUS
DECEPTION

For Alan—
with love and fond memories of Monaco.

CHAPTER ONE

THE tread of confident footsteps echoed across the sun-warmed tiles of the terrace—the tread of a man whose presence spelled danger.

Even without turning around, Rayne guessed who he was and could sense a desire in him to unnerve her.

No, it was more of a determination, she decided, with every cell alert, tensing from the fear of being recognised—an assurance that whatever this man wanted, this man got.

'So you're the little waif my father plucked off the street, who's showing her gratitude by deigning to drive him around.'

She had been looking, from her vantage point through the balconied archway, out over coral-coloured blocks of high-rise apartments, some with roof gardens, others with pools that seemed to throw back fire from the setting sun. But now she ignored the glittering sea, the palace on The Rock and the sun-streaked cliffs that were a feature of this coast—but particularly of this rich man's playground that was Monte Carlo—swinging round instead with her blazing hair falling heavily over one shoulder and her body stiffening from the derisory undertones of the deep English voice.

His clothes were tailored to perfection. And expensive, Rayne decided grudgingly. From his pristine white shirt and dark designer suit, to the very tip of his shiny black shoes. A man whose cool, sophisticated image masked a deceptively ruthless nature and a tongue that could cut with the deftness of a scythe.

For a moment she couldn't speak, stunned by how the years had given him such a powerful presence. Recent newspaper photographs, she realised, had failed to capture the striking quality about him that owed less to his stunning classic features and thick black hair that had a tendency to fall across his forehead than to that breath-catching aura that seemed to surround his tall, muscular frame.

'For your information, I'm twenty-five.'

Why had she told him that? Because of the condescending way in which he had referred to her? Or to assure him that she was a woman now and not the shrieking eighteen-year-old he had had to deal with that last time they had met.

The cock of a deprecating eyebrow told her he had taken her response in the way that his calculating brain evidently wanted to. That she was more than eligible to bed his father, and that she was probably planning to do so—if she hadn't already—with purely mercenary motives in mind. But there wasn't a glimmer of recognition in those steel-blue eyes...

'And he didn't pluck me off the street,' she corrected him, allowing herself to relax a little. 'We were both victims of a spiteful ploy to relieve me of my possessions. I came to France—and then Monaco—for a break, and I was left with no credit cards, no money and nowhere to stay.' Why did she feel she had to justify herself to him? she thought with her jaw clenching. Because she hadn't been sitting in that pavement café just by coincidence? Because as an experienced journalist who had researched her subject thoroughly beforehand, she knew exactly where Mitchell Clayborne would be? 'Your father very kindly offered me a roof over my head until I could get things sorted out.'

That wide masculine mouth she had always thought of as passionate compressed in a rather judgemental fashion. 'A bit remiss of you not to have booked ahead.'

Why did every word he uttered sound like an accusation? Or was it just guilt making her imagine things? The dread of being found out?

'My mother's been ill for the past year or so. Now her condition's stabilised she took up her friend's offer to go away for three weeks, and so I decided to just take off.' It had seemed like a good idea from the security of the little rented Victorian house she still shared with her mother in London, although she knew that Cynthia Hardwicke would have thrown up her hands in horror if she knew the real reason her daughter was taking this trip. 'I had somewhere to stay until that morning.' She shrugged and didn't think it worth bothering to tell him that her friend, Joanne, who now lived in the South of France with her husband, and whom she'd been planning to spend some time with, had been unexpectedly descended upon by her sister and her three young nieces, so that Rayne had had to politely offer to move on before she was asked. 'With the holiday season barely started, I didn't envisage too much problem checking in somewhere.' Except that she hadn't reckoned on being robbed before she'd got the chance. 'I'd hired a car for the day, stopped for a coffee and…well… you obviously know the rest.'

He knew what his father had told him, but Mitch was clearly biased, King thought, and he could see why. Despite referring to her as 'little' just now, this woman was—what? Five feet six? Five seven?—with a good figure. And quite striking, too, with that Titian red hair. Or did they call that auburn? Her skin was creamy, complementing big eyes set just wide enough apart for his liking and a particularly full mouth a man could easily get carried away by. And there was certainly nothing waiflike about that air of confidence about her which, being as shrewd a judge of people as he was, did seem rather too assertive for a woman without an agenda. He wondered what that agenda could be, as he recalled how Mitch had said he'd picked her up.

Apparently his father had been leaving his usual lunch venue last Wednesday, alone because, as cantankerous as ever, Mitch had that morning had a barney with the latest chauffeur King had engaged for him and sent the man packing.

Rigid to routine, it was typical of Mitch that he'd refused to change his plans or wait for another member of staff to drive him into town, and had taken the old Bentley—which had been modified for him to use—himself. Not that he thought his father wasn't capable. But it was inadvisable for a sixty-seven-year-old man of Mitch's prominence to be out without proper security, even for one who wasn't so physically challenged. After transferring himself into the car—always a struggle for him—outside the café and folding up his wheelchair, the wheel he'd taken off was snatched from under his nose in broad daylight. It just went to show how susceptible he was. It also proved how easily his stubborn independence could be taken from him, and would have been if this supposedly ministering angel King saw before him hadn't leapt up and given chase.

He affected an air of effortless charm. 'It seems I should be thanking you for looking out for my father, Miss…'

'Carpenter. Rayne Carpenter.'

It wasn't her real name. Well, not entirely. It was her mother's maiden name and the name Rayne had used in the small provincial newspaper she used to write for. But then introducing herself as Lorrayne Hardwicke would only have earned her a one-way ticket out of there, she thought with a little shiver, even though she had been planning to tell his father exactly who she was in the beginning. At first…before those thieves had intervened and thrown all her well-laid plans awry.

'You're the best reporter I have, but you've got to come up with a story!' her editor had told her six months ago, before he'd been forced to let her go when her mother's worrying illness and inevitable operation had forced her to take too much time off.

Well, she could come up with a story! she thought now, with her teeth clamped almost painfully together. It was one exposé she wanted, and one everyone would want to read. Except that this one was personal...

She saw a muscle twitch in the man's hard angular jaw as he came closer—close enough for her to catch the scent of his cologne—as fresh as the pines that clothed the steeply rising hillside.

'I'm Kingsley Clayborne. But everyone calls me King,' he told her, holding out a hand.

I know who you are!

Her confidence wavered. She didn't want to touch him. But fear of his checking up on her if she showed any sign of unease or aversion to him forced her to plaster on a bright smile. Taking the hand he was offering, she found herself responding before she could stop herself, 'I'll bet they do!'

Feeling her slender hand tremble in his, King let his fingers find a subtle path across the blue vein pulsing in her wrist. He noted the way it was throbbing in double-quick tempo. There was something about her eyes too. Deep hazel eyes flecked with green, which were darkly guarded as they fixed on his. But fix on them they did, with a contention that was as challenging as it was wary, and which mirrored the superficial smile on her beautiful bronze-tinted mouth.

He knew his father could take care of himself. He was a man of the world, for heaven's sake! But Mitch was also vulnerable to a pretty face, and therefore to unscrupulous gold-diggers—and this Rayne Carpenter was one hell of a cagey lady.

Even so, he wasn't blind to the long, elegant line of her pale, translucent throat, or the way it contracted nervously beneath his blatant regard. Any more than he could fail to notice that her breasts—the cleft of which was just tantalisingly visible above the neckline of her chic but simple black dress—were high and generously proportioned. Quite a handful, in fact.

Hell! He was surprised by how acutely his body responded to the femininity she seemed to flaunt without any conscious effort, especially when his keen mind was telling him that Miss Rayne Carpenter was definitely one to watch. But there was something about her...

Some memory tugged at his subconscious like the fragment of a dream, too elusive to grasp, but still powerful enough to deepen the crease between his thick, winged brows, compelling him to enquire, 'Have we met before?'

Beads of perspiration broke out over Rayne's body, as tangible as that strong hand that was clasping hers, prickling above her top lip and along the deep V between her breasts.

She gave a nervous little laugh and said, 'I hardly think so.'

She wasn't sure whether he had let her go or whether she had been the one to break the contact, but as her hand slipped out of his she realised that she was desperate to take a breath.

Deep inside her something stirred. Resentment? Dislike? What else could have produced this overwhelming reaction to him that had her blood surging, not just from his question, but from the unwelcome and disturbing touch of his hand? After all, anything she might have felt for him he had killed off a long time ago, she assured herself caustically. But it had been more than a touch, she reasoned, despising him—as well as herself—for the way he was making her feel.

With one simple handshake she felt as though she'd been assessed, undressed and bedded by him, because behind that probing scrutiny that had trapped the breath in her lungs there had been a fundamental appreciation of a man for a woman. Yet there was still no sign of recognition...

Her breath, marked with trembling relief, shivered shallowly through her when he accepted her denial of having met him before. But then everyone she met nowadays who hadn't seen her since she was a teenager remarked on how much she had changed. Seven years ago she had had no real curves and her hair had been short and spiky, as well as a different colour. And back then, of course, she would simply have been known as Lorri…

'Those thieves must have reckoned on your being a definite pushover, don't you think?' he remarked smoothly. 'For the three of them to have targeted you so precisely?'

She took a step back, finding his dominating presence much too stifling, his question baffling her even as it warned her to be on her guard. 'I'm sorry…?'

'I mean that they must have noticed you taking more than a passing interest in my father to be so certain you'd rise to their bait when they took that wheel and rush off and help him as you did.'

Could he hear her heart hammering away inside her?

'I don't like seeing anyone taken advantage of,' she said pointedly, and then, with barely concealed venom, 'for any reason.' Now, with her head cocked to one side, she demanded, 'What exactly are you insinuating, Mr—'

'King.'

Perhaps 'Your Majesty' would please you more!

She had to bite her lower lip to stop from crying it aloud. He was rich and powerful now. As well as ruthless, she decided bitterly.

Even then, all those years ago, when she'd crashed in on the ugly scene between him and her father, she had seen a side to him she hadn't realised he'd possessed. A steel edge to his personality, coupled with a determined lack of scruples for a young man who, while still only twenty-three, had been forced, through his father's accident, to learn the ropes quickly so that he could pick up the reins of a company about to explode on the world.

'I couldn't help but take an interest in him—or in what he was doing, certainly!' she breathed now, hating him for the part he had played in destroying her father, while warning herself that nothing would escape this man's notice or bypass the keen circuits of his cold, intellectual mind. 'I was struck by the way he'd overcome his obvious difficulties to be able to drive himself around like that. I wasn't aware that admiring someone's capabilities actually constituted a crime.'

'It doesn't.' His smile seemed to light his face like the evening sun lit the rooftops of Monte Carlo, leaving her struck by its transformation from a dark enigma to one of pure blinding charm.

Rayne's throat worked nervously. Was he backing off?

'As you've probably been told, my father's chauffeur left... rather suddenly. Hence the reason he was without a driver, although, I should say, thanks to you, that that breach has been miraculously filled.'

She nodded, ignoring the sarcasm lacing his words.

Her heavy hair moved softly around her shoulders, King noticed, the warmth of the evening light turning it to flame.

His thick black eyelashes came down as he followed the rivers of fire to where they ended just above her contrastingly pale breasts. 'I gather you didn't lose everything at the hands of those criminals.' A toss of his chin indicated the clothes she was wearing, but the way those appraising blue eyes slid down her quivering body invested even that innocuous statement with disturbing sensuality.

'My clothes were in my car.'

'And they didn't take your keys?'

'No. They were in my jeans pocket.' With her cellphone, she thought—mercifully!—although she didn't tell King that. She had taken it out of her bag to text her mother just minutes before Mitchell Clayborne had emerged from the hotel restaurant next to the café the other day, and she had been immensely relieved that she had. It meant that she had been able to cancel her credit and debit cards and report the crime to the police in the privacy of the hired car, while leaving her cellphone number with them in case of any developments—so nobody would be ringing and asking for Lorrayne Hardwicke on her host's landline.

Tilting her head, she viewed the formidably attractive heir of Clayborne International with her throat dry from a raw sexual awareness and enquired, 'Do you interrogate all your father's house guests like this?'

His mouth tugged on one side as he moved over to the granite-topped table on the terrace and poured himself some coffee from the silver pot a manservant had brought out a little while ago. A masculine hand—long-fingered and tanned—queried whether he should pour some for her.

Rayne shook her head, dragging her gaze from the stark contrast of an immaculate white cuff and dark wrist to note that he added no cream or sugar to his cup.

'But you're not just a house guest, are you?' he remarked wryly. 'You've insisted on working while you're here until you get your affairs straightened out, which makes you an employee of sorts—albeit a rather unconventional one—and my father doesn't engage anyone these days without consulting me.'

And that just showed who was ruling the Clayborne empire now, she thought, resenting the authority he exuded as well as that brooding magnetism and forcefulness of character that lent his features a strength and quality that went way beyond mere handsomeness. 'You must excuse me if you think I'm being overly cautious.' She watched him drink through the steam rising from his cup and then set the fine china down on the table with cool economical movements. 'But, as I'm sure you're aware, my father is a very wealthy man.'

So are you, she supplied silently, remembering how amazed she had been to read that article that reported him as being higher up Britain's Rich List last year even than Mitchell Clayborne. That it was at her father's expense that the Claybornes were in that enviable position was something she refused to dwell on. She was aware, though, of the numerous enterprises King was involved in outside their technological empire, and reluctantly accepted that a man of his drive and determination would succeed at anything he turned his hand to. She looked at him askance and with a confrontational note in her voice queried, 'Meaning?'

He made a careless gesture with his hands. 'A beautiful young woman. An obviously rich but vulnerable older man whose ego needs a bit of boosting. An unlikely prank-turned-robbery in the midst of a crowded café. You must admit it couldn't be a more finely tuned scheme to play on the older man's sympathies and to get you into this house if you'd engineered it yourself.'

The colour already touching her cheeks intensified on a surge of guilt because, of course, she had been waiting at that table specifically for his father's appearance, but not for the reasons his sceptical guard dog of a son was suggesting!

Still trying to deny the heat coursing through her veins from his remark about her being beautiful, she retorted, 'That's preposterous!'

'Is it?' He slipped a hand into his trouser pocket, bringing her attention unwillingly to the hard lean line of his pelvis until, shocked at where she was looking, she dropped her gaze down over his intimidating stance and long, long legs. 'It isn't unheard of.'

'Except for one thing, King.' They both glanced in the direction of the shaky, gravelly voice, accompanied now by the unmistakable squeak of the wheelchair approaching. 'She didn't want to come.'

It was true. She hadn't at first. When those thieves had left her with nothing but a car with a virtually empty fuel tank, no money or credit and no place to stay, she had been uncomfortable enough with Mitchell Clayborne's gratitude for returning his property without his offer of assistance when he realised the loss and inconvenience that helping him had caused her. After all, she'd been lying in wait for him solely for one reason: to confront him with who she was and to threaten him if necessary with exposure in the papers if he didn't come clean and admit the wrong that both he and King had done to her father. To try and prick his conscience—if he had one!—where Grant Hardwicke had failed, because Mitch Clayborne and his son had taken something more precious from her family than a simple wheel! But he'd seemed so shaken up by those morons running off with it that it hadn't been the time or the place. Besides, she'd only been waiting at that café because she knew she would never have got past this villa's impregnable security if she had tried to see him here, so, after her initial hesitation, she'd decided to grab the opportunity she was being offered with both hands.

After all, the Claybornes owed her family big time, she'd decided, and all she had to do was bide her time until she had got her credit cards sorted out, enjoy a bit of luxury for a night or two and then, when her host was feeling better, she'd come clean and tell him who she really was. But it hadn't worked out like that.

'Hear that, King?' Mitchell Clayborne brought his chair out into the scented dusky air, warm still even though the light was fading. His iron-grey hair, combed straight back, was still thick like his son's, but his face was more harshly etched as his lined blue eyes clashed with the brooding intensity of the younger man's. 'I said she didn't want to come.'

Despite the gathering shadows around the pale stonework of the house, Rayne saw a fragment of a smile pull at King's sensual mouth.

'Your discretion becomes you,' he remarked quietly. His eyes said something quite different, though, she was sure, as they swept over her tight, tense features—as did the scarcely concealed scepticism with which he spoke.

Did he know? she wondered with her heart banging against her ribs. Had he guessed who she was and was just playing with her? Or did his only beef about her stem from the fact that she hadn't come through his stringent security system? Been passed to him first for his cold and calculating assessment?

'Leave her alone, King.' Mitchell was pushing himself over to the table as King reached for the cut glass decanter beside the coffee pot and poured some of its golden contents into a matching tumbler. 'Can't I enjoy a bit of female company without you vetting her like she was some filly with a dubious pedigree?' Mitch took the glass from the man who was more than thirty-five years his junior, and yet whose influence and power in the corporate world was more respected and deferred to even than the older man's these days.

King's shoulder lifted and a sudden last shaft of sunlight, piercing through the trees that decked the hillsides, splintered colour from the crystal decanter in his hand. 'Of course.' Replacing its stopper, he put the decanter back on the table with a dull thud. 'But be it on your own head, Mitch. I'm not going to be riding this one.'

Rayne's back stiffened from the double entendre as she watched him walk away, looking every bit as proud as the man in the wheelchair, but exuding an air of such uncompromising autonomy that lesser men, including his own father, could only hope to aspire to.

'He doesn't like me,' Rayne observed dryly, her confident manner concealing how uncomfortably sticky he'd made her feel beneath her light clothes. Had he picked up on the fact that she was hiding something from them? Or was her guilty secret letting her imagination run away with her?

'You'll have to excuse my son. He suspects every woman who happens to give me the time of day,' Mitch told her. 'Especially if she's young and pretty. Usually he manages to frighten them off before the dust has time to settle under their feet.'

'That's pretty selfish of him.' Rayne's eyes lingered in

the direction the other man had gone, her jaw tightening in rebellion.

'He has no reason to be. With a physical and intellectual package like that, they all wind up wanting King anyway.' He gave a harsh bark of laughter. 'Well, who would want an old fossil like me?' He started to cough, the contents of his glass threatening to slop over the side. As Rayne moved forward to take it from him, he waved her impatiently aside. 'But what's a man to do?' The terrace lights had come on, taking over from the sun that had dipped behind the mountains and glinting on the crystal he lifted to his mouth, draining it in one swift gulp. 'He calls it protecting my interests. Here—' he thrust the empty glass in her direction '—pour me another one, will you?'

Rayne looked at him dubiously. He was already looking rather florid. She'd also learned from his late-middle-aged and amiable Swiss housekeeper while she'd been there that Mitchell Clayborne had high blood pressure as well as a heart condition, which was why Rayne had been hesitant to tell him who she was and why she was there. 'Do you think you should?'

'For heaven's sake, girl! You have the audacity to question my actions while you're a guest in my house?'

'I didn't mean to.' Nor did she want to find herself worrying over someone who had treated her father so abominably. It felt like a betrayal, somehow. But her father's ex-colleague and business partner seemed world-weary and surprisingly bitter, she had decided over the past few days, guessing that it was probably because of his disability, although having an heir as forceful and dynamic as King couldn't help. But she was getting used to her host's outbursts, startling though they were, and so she took the glass he was handing her and poured him another drink.

'You're behaving just like King,' he persisted. 'And while

he's excused through blood, I won't take it from anyone who isn't. D'you understand?'

'Perfectly,' she breathed with mock deference as she handed him his refill, and caught a surprising glint of warmth in his watery blue eyes. 'If you don't need anything else,' she tagged on, uncomfortable even with fraternizing with him because of what he had done in the past, 'I think I'll get an early night.'

He smiled, gesturing her away with his glass, his angry mood dispelled. 'Good idea. Oh, Rayne...' Stopping before the open door that separated the luxurious living quarters from the terrace, she turned round with the scent of a potted gardenia trespassing on her senses. 'About King... Did you do something to antagonise him before I came out?'

Her heart skipped a nervous little beat. 'No. Why?'

'I haven't seen him quite so...intense before.'

She shrugged, trying to shake off the feeling of exposure she had sensed under those steely-blue eyes, trying not to remember how she had felt in the past. 'Perhaps he had a hard day.'

'Nonsense. He thrives on hard work and pressure where lesser mortals crack up and fall by the wayside.'

'He sounds like a dynamo.'

'He is.'

'Even dynamos can break down.'

'If you think that, then you don't know King.'

Don't I? she thought bitterly, but said, 'Obviously not.'

'But you will,' he said, seemingly with some relish. 'He's going to be around for a while.'

'That's nice.' She was finding it difficult keeping her voice light, making out that she didn't care one way or the other, while her insides were screaming with guilt and resentment and a whole heap of worrying doubts over what she was getting herself into.

'And Rayne...' About to step inside, keen to escape to her

room, Rayne glanced reluctantly over her shoulder as Mitch called to her again. 'Be nice to him,' he advised with just a hint of caution. 'For both our sakes.'

I'll fall at his feet, shall I? she suggested silently. *Like I'm sure every nubile woman he meets probably does!*

Her face ached from her forced smile as she got out, 'Of course,' aware that she was suddenly in danger of finding herself in way over her head, even as she told herself that she refused to be intimidated by King's arrival. He might look like the stuff of every woman's dreams, she accepted grudgingly, as the spacious interior of his father's summer retreat, which had astounded her with its elegance and luxury ever since she'd been there, now felt as though it was swallowing her up. And if just a compliment from him or the most casual of physical contact—like shaking hands with him, for goodness' sake!—made her pulse quicken a bit…well…it was only her hormones working, wasn't it? She was only human, after all! But she'd come to Monaco to try to right the wrong that had been done to her father and she had no intention of letting a man like King—or her uncontrollable hormones— stand in her way!

CHAPTER TWO

THE shapes and tones and hues of Monte Carlo took her breath away, as they had been doing every time she'd looked down on them from her bedroom balcony over the past few days. But this morning, with the sun still low enough to have turned the sea to gold and wrapped the distant mountains in a haze of heat, this wakening resort seemed, like her, to be holding its breath, before offering up its vibrant heart to another day of wealth and glamour and total luxury.

Rayne grimaced at the comparison because she hadn't come to Monaco to indulge herself. But while she was here, she thought, noticing how the trees on the steep ascent of the hillside above the house were touched with the same flame gold as the water in the harbour, then at least she could appreciate the scenery.

The only blot on her immediate horizon, she decided, was King.

She'd been careful before she'd embarked on this trip to do a little research into where he would be, and right now he should have been attending some week-long charity function in New York. After all, King didn't live here. He had some luxurious pad in London, and she'd heard that he and his father didn't always see eye to eye.

What he was doing here, she didn't know, only that it was going to be difficult enough confronting Mitch with who she was and why she was there, but with that six-foot-something of potent manhood thrown into the mix, the prospect was no less than unnerving.

He was hard, ruthless and clever. He was also suspicious, which left her feeling as though every secret she harboured was under threat of being exposed to him, while every feminine cell in her body reacted to his raw sexuality with a strength that left her shocked and ashamed.

She'd thought such wild reactions were the predilection of teenage girls. Because he had affected her then—seven years ago—although he'd scarcely spared more than a passing glance her way. A wheat-blonde, spiky-haired teenager with purple-shadowed eyes and lipstick. An experimental and pathetic Lorri Hardwicke, whose nevertheless deeply buried secret had been an excruciating crush on the firm's youngest and most dynamic recruit who, not long out of university, was already being primed for directorship.

She had wanted him from the first instant she had nearly collided with him as he was coming out of the office one day when she had been meeting her father for lunch, and from that moment she had woven all sorts of wild fantasies around him.

Young and guileless and between jobs, introduced to him only briefly, she'd jumped at the chance to help out in the office for a couple of weeks when one of the typists was on leave. It had offered her a chance to be near King, after all. But he'd scarcely spoken to her and, like Mitch, he had spent a lot of time out of the office. And when he was there she'd watched him from a painful distance behind her frosted glass partition, imagining a golden future when he would suddenly realise she was there, waiting in the wings for him to notice her, ask her out and initiate her into the sophisticated art of making love. Because with a man like him, she had decided, without any doubt in her fixated young mind, lovemaking would be no less than an art.

Even after she'd left, she still kept hoping. That was until the evening he had come round to the house and shattered all her dreams. Made her hate him with an emotion all the more intense because of what it had replaced.

Bitterly her thoughts drifted back to that night seven years ago. It was just a few weeks after her father had had a row with Mitchell Clayborne and walked away from their partnership—with devastating repercussions.

She had been to the gym and had cycled home in the rain, coming in to hear raised voices, her father's thin and defensive, King's deep and inexorable.

'You're the thief, Grant Hardwicke! Not my father! Stay away from him. Do I make myself clear? Leave him alone or you'll have me to deal with!' It still made her shudder to remember his cruel, icy threat. 'Believe me, after this you won't know what hit you if you ever dare show your face at our house or at the office again!'

Towering over Grant Hardwicke, King had been standing in the hallway of the modern detached home her mother had so prized, while her father had seemed to visibly diminish before Rayne's eyes. His features blanched and strained, she had seen Grant grab the doorframe as though it was too much of an effort to support himself under the weight of the younger man's hostile and verbal attack.

Soaked to the skin, hair flattened by the rain, she'd flown at King like a drenched sparrow as he'd come striding back across the hall.

'Don't you dare hurt my father!' she'd sobbed, lashing out at him, her flailing fists ineffectual against the impenetrable wall of his body. 'I'll kill you first! I will! I'll kill you!'

'Calm down, Lorri…' He had referred to her by name. It was the first time she could remember him using it, much less showing her any attention, but then it had been only to catch her flying wrists and thrust her aside as if she were an unwanted toy. 'Don't waste your hysterics and your childish little threats on me,' he'd warned with particular brutality to her teenage pride. 'Save them for someone who deserves them,' he'd snarled savagely. 'Like your father!' He had slammed out of the door with his hurtful and puzzling words burning in her ears.

'It's about that software, love,' Grant Hardwicke had breathed brokenly when she had rushed over to him. He'd looked drained and exhausted as she'd helped him onto an easy chair. 'Mitchell's saying it's company property and King's backing him up. I'm afraid they're determined to keep it. I've lost everything, Lorri. *Everything.*' She had never forgotten the desperation in her father's voice.

'But it's yours, Dad. You wrote it!' Rayne remembered stressing, as though that had counted for anything where the Clayborne men were concerned. It was software he had written especially for the medical profession. One he had said would benefit a lot of people—because her father was like that—caring and generous. It was something he had produced for the common good. It was his baby. His brainchild, which he'd conceived and worked on and slaved over in his own time before he had ever joined forces with Mitchell Clayborne. But Mitchell Clayborne had stolen the credit for it, launching it under his own company flag with the full knowledge and support of his equally unscrupulous and ambitious son and heir.

Her mother had been out at a line-dancing class that night and Rayne was glad she had because it was the first and only time in her life she had seen her father cry. Her strong and devoted father, who had always been her rock and the backbone of his family, reduced to tears in losing all he'd worked for. But he had no proof of his copyright for that software he had written, and the Claybornes had gone on to prosper unbelievably because of it, while Grant Hardwicke's troubles had only increased.

Because of his age, he had found it impossible to get another position. He'd started drinking, which made him ill, and then he was made bankrupt, which in turn meant her mother having to lose her lovely home.

Rayne was certain that all her father's problems had started that night she had walked in on King's unmitigated venom. A venom that had had a poisoning effect on her family, virtually destroying everything that had been good about it, everything she'd loved.

What she had felt for him had been unreal, Rayne thought bitterly, mocking herself now. A teenage fancy, as insubstantial as mist, killed off by his pulsing anger and his verbal brutality towards her father, even before she'd realised how unscrupulous he was. As well as defending Grant, she knew now that in striking King that night she had been giving vent to the loss of all her young dreams. But long after the anguish of that night had receded, it was the physical power of him and those firm hands on her body as he'd put her from him that had lingered in her memory...

She came downstairs now with half a hope that, in spite of what Mitch had said, perhaps his son's visit might have been a flying one and that he might have been called away on some vital company business during the night.

That was until she saw him striding in through the front door in a short-sleeved white shirt that exposed his tanned, muscular arms and dark suit trousers hugging his powerful hips and her heart seemed to stand still before vaulting into a double-quick rhythm.

'Good morning, Rayne.' He was tie-less, she realised, with her gaze instantly drawn to the bronze skin beneath his corded throat. The white T-shirt she had teamed with her jeans suddenly felt too snug for her breasts as that steely gaze burned over her. 'I trust you slept well.'

She hadn't, but she said in a tight little voice, 'Very, thank you.' In fact she had been waking up all night, going over that scenario with him on the terrace, aware that it was absolutely imperative that she confront his father about that software before King had a chance to work out who she was.

Consequently, the bruised-eyed-looking creature who had

stared back at her from the mirror this morning as she'd swept her hair up into a loose knot left her feeling quite bedraggled in contrast to King, who looked as fresh and energized as the morning and ready to take the world on those wide, powerful shoulders.

'You'll be pleased to know you won't have to drive my father into town as you were planning to do this morning,' he said smoothly, those keen eyes seeming to assess her every reaction. 'He decided to leave early and, as I was up, I drove him in myself.'

The front door was open and she could see the huge bulk of the Bentley parked there on the drive. A short distance away, the sleeker, more powerful beast of a black Lamborghini stood gleaming in the bright morning sun.

'You didn't need to do that. I mean…' her eyes strayed towards the carved wooden door concealing the lift that would have borne Mitch down in his wheelchair. '…he should have called me.'

'Oh, I think I did.'

Meaning what? Rayne's throat contracted nervously from the way he was looking at her. That he was protecting his father from her supposedly mercenary clutches? Or was his sole intention to get her alone? And, if so, why? To interrogate her further?

Mentally, she pulled back her shoulders, telling herself that he was just trying to unsettle her. That he'd hardly be likely to discover the truth about her just so long as she kept her head.

'In that case…' she flashed him what she considered would look like a grateful smile '…I'll go and get some breakfast.'

'I think you might be disappointed there.'

Stopping in her tracks, she glanced up at him with her brow furrowing. 'Excuse me?'

'I instructed Hélène not to bother. I've given her the morning off.'

A cloud of wariness darkened the green flecks in her eyes.

Why had he done that? Had he realised who she was and was planning on giving her marching orders while his father was out of the way?

A smile illuminated his strong features like the sun burning through the haze of the mountains she'd been admiring earlier, making her pulse quicken in infuriating response. 'As it was such a lovely morning I thought I'd have breakfast out. I also thought you might care to join me.'

Oh, did he?

'No, really. That's very nice of you,' she blurted out, even though 'nice' was definitely not a word she would have applied to Kingsley Clayborne, 'but…'

But what, exactly? She couldn't claim she never ate breakfast after what she had just told him. Nor could she inform him that she didn't like him, and that if she had to choose between sharing breakfast with him or with a pride of lions, she'd take the pride of lions.

'I…I need to stay here for when your father needs to be picked up,' she hedged, wishing she didn't sound so defensive.

'He won't. Not until later. If you haven't discovered it yet, you'll soon learn that my father is a creature of unwavering habit. Always reliable, but sometimes tiresomely predictable.' Which was how she had managed to meet him that day outside that café. 'He's doing some business and then playing chess with a friend and won't be ready to come home until mid-afternoon. Any change in those plans and he'll ring me. That's settled then,' he declared when she procrastinated too long, having run out of reasonable excuses. 'And I can assure you…' his tone had changed in a way that sent a cautioning little shiver through her '…I'm not trying to be nice.'

'I'm glad you told me.' She sent another forced smile over her shoulder as she obeyed his gesture for her to precede him through the front door.

'No,' he called out as she moved towards the Bentley, 'we'll take mine.'

A skein of unease uncoiled in Rayne's stomach after she'd crossed the tarmac and pulled the door of the Lamborghini closed behind her.

This sleek and powerful machine with its cream leather-scented interior represented major success. Arrival. It was also Kingsley Clayborne's territory. With its smooth engineering wrapped around her and the cushioning curves of the passenger seat seeming to suck her in, she felt uncomfortably under his influence, as though her own power and control had suddenly been considerably reduced.

'Relax,' he advised, sensing her tension, obviously thinking it stemmed from something else altogether, she realised, when he tagged on, 'I might be renowned for my love of power, but I'm not altogether insensitive to those riding alongside me.'

Was that what he thought? That she was afraid of how fast he might drive this thing? Or was he talking about a different kind of power altogether? Because she didn't doubt that he enjoyed being in command. Of himself. Of others. And of his multi-billion, multi-national company. Because, where the Clayborne empire was concerned, it was common knowledge that he had been the one taking all the major decisions for some years now.

'I'm pleased to hear it,' she said, her voice overly bright, and kept her eyes trained on the panoramic views from the window on her side so that they wouldn't stray to the movement of muscle beneath the dark cloth spanning his thigh, or be pulled by the flash of gold from the slim watch on his wrist as he changed gear with that masculine hand.

'It's stunning, isn't it?' he remarked, aware, as her eyes drank in the scenery from the awe-inspiring sweep of the road. A road that ran all the way along the French Riviera to the Italian coast, she remembered reading from a travel brochure before she'd left England. Someone had called it the most romantic road in the world.

Feeling as though the Lamborghini were a bird and that they were travelling on its wings, they soared above terracotta-roofed houses dotted amongst tree-smothered cliffs, above church spires and tumbling hillsides that plunged down to the rugged coastline and the sea.

Above them the Alps presided, white-capped and as ageless as time. And just a little bit unnerving, Rayne decided, although not as unnerving as when King suddenly pulled into a surprisingly deserted lay-by. Her mind raced with the instinctive knowledge that Kingsley Clayborne would never do anything without a reason, and that that reason wasn't just to enjoy the view.

'What are you imagining?' he enquired mockingly, wise to the half-wary, half-questioning look she shot him. 'That I brought you up here to seduce you?'

She gave a tight little laugh. 'No. Why? Did you?'

Dear heaven! Had she actually said that? Obviously her nerves were getting the better of her, she thought, in letting her tongue run away with her.

He laughed. 'No.' The engine died under the portentous turn of the ignition key. 'Of course, if you were hoping I was...'

Every nerve in her body seemed to pull like overstretched rubber bands. There was a time, she thought, when she was young and blinded by his looks and his devastating persona, that her heart would have leapt in wild anticipation of what he might be planning, not thumping in screaming rejection as it was doing now. Or was it? she startled herself by wondering suddenly, deciding not to go there.

Turning to him with her cheeks scorched scarlet, she said pointedly, 'Are you always so sure of yourself?'

He laughed again, under his breath this time. 'Are you?'

Her own question, lobbed back at her, left her speechless for a moment.

With his bent elbow on the steering wheel, a thumb and

forefinger supporting his chin, his thick lashes were drawn down as he studied her reflectively, giving her every ounce of his attention. Dear heaven! What she wouldn't have given for this much attention from him seven years ago!

Berating herself for even thinking along those lines, unable to meet his eyes, she still couldn't stop herself appreciating his classic and magnificent bone structure, the chiselled sweep of his forehead and cheekbones, that proud flaring nose, that tantalising dent in his chin...

'I'm just finding it hard,' he expressed, shocking her back to her senses, 'determining why any woman would accept a strange man's hospitality—even if he is driving a Bentley—unless she's either very foolish or hoping to gain something out of it.'

Of course. Rayne bit the inside of her cheek.

'I suppose in normal circumstances I wouldn't even have considered it,' she told him, finding her tongue. 'But in view of his age and the fact that he said he had a house full of staff to look after me, I thought I'd be perfectly safe.'

'And were you aware of who he was?' he enquired. 'Before he brought you home with him?'

Rayne's heartbeat increased. Be careful, she warned herself. He doesn't know who you are. Just breathe normally. Keep your cool.

'I knew the name, certainly...as soon as he said it.' She gave a nonchalant little shrug. 'Who wouldn't? Who doesn't know the name of the man who gave MiracleMed to a grateful medical profession?' It was an effort to smile. To pretend to believe what everyone else believed about Mitchell Clayborne. 'He's a very clever man.'

That firm mouth twisted contemplatively. Such a cruel yet sensual mouth, she decided, in spite of her dislike of its owner. Crazily, she wondered how many women had felt the pressure of it, known the power of this man's unrestrained passion.

'Yes,' he breathed, 'but I meant before those delinquents sidetracked you into chasing after them.'

Rayne gave herself a mental shake. What the hell was she thinking about? she berated herself.

Unconsciously now, she brought her tongue across her top lip. She hated lying, even on her father's account. 'Are you still suggesting I planned for someone to rob me so I could play on your father's sympathies and wheedle my way into his house for some financial benefit?' she queried, her voice cracking slightly because she wasn't being straight with him, even if it was for reasons other than he was implying. 'If you think I'm interested in your father's money, then all I can say is you've got a very overstretched imagination!'

He laughed softly, unperturbed by the rising note in her voice.

'And I could suggest that the reason you don't like women taking an interest in your father,' she went on heatedly, with a sudden surge of pity for Mitchell Clayborne that surprised her, 'is because you might lose all *you* stand to gain if he reciprocates!'

'Hardly,' he said with a tug of that sensuous mouth.

Because he was involved in so many other enterprises besides the company his father had founded and in which her own father had played such a major part, a man of King's calibre, determination and unwavering command, she accepted rather grudgingly, didn't need to rely on anyone or anything, least of all the prospect of inherited wealth.

'Let's eat,' he said, restarting the engine, the cutting edge of his gaze picking up on the way her lovely breasts rose and fell.

But with what? he wondered. Relief?

As his success depended on his keen ability to sense any subtle changes in mood or behaviour—both in his business rivals and in his own workforce—his experience had served him well, and it didn't let him down now.

Rayne Carpenter portrayed all the characteristics of a woman who wasn't being entirely honest, he decided, pulling away. And yet what could she be hiding if it wasn't a very determined plan of action to ensnare Mitch? He had seen his father preyed upon before—several times—but once in particular, and with disastrous consequences, and he'd be hanged if he'd stand by and let Mitch bring such devastation down on himself again.

No, he decided, with sudden inexorable purpose. The thing he had to do was to keep her away from his father—at least until he could check her out. And the best way to do that was to claim all this dubious young woman's time for himself.

He had some time on his hands as his second-in-command had taken over his commitments in the States, and he had already promised himself a short break when it was over. He had never had any difficulty seducing any woman he put his mind to seducing, and with this one, he decided grimly, conscience didn't even come into it. If she was the sort of woman who was out just to prey on Mitch, then the prospect of even richer pickings with him should get her opportunistic juices flowing nicely.

It was an unfortunate choice of words, and one which was making his mind work overtime as he imagined her hot and compliant, moist with the honeyed heat of desire. He felt his body's hard response as he imagined freeing those beautiful breasts from their restricting cups and moulding them to his hands, feeling each sensitive tip blossom as he took it into his mouth.

He shook away his errant fantasies, trying to pull himself together. It was probably because he hadn't had a woman in his bed for some months, he decided, that his body was behaving like a rampant adolescent's now. Still, he couldn't deny that the prospect of stripping this unsuspecting little gold-digger bare—and in more ways than one—excited him immensely.

The café to which he took her was situated in a pedestrian thoroughfare, paved in the same peach and cream tones as the buildings which flanked it. Baskets of flowers—red and purple and pink—decorated ornamental street lamps, while luxuriant foliage grew in abundance outside the shops and cafés. There were orange trees, Rayne recognised, growing beneath the artistically wrought balconies of the buildings, whose pastel-coloured shutters and breath-catching architecture were a testament to human creativity, in contrast to the awesome cliffs that formed a mighty backdrop behind the buildings that stood at the head of the elegant avenue.

'Here we are,' King invited, pulling out a chair for her, the smile he gave her appreciative of her wonderment in spite of what he had been thinking about her earlier.

A little later, drinking coffee with home-baked rolls spread thickly with locally made jam, Rayne was relieved when King's conversation touched only on things like the area and the recent airways strike. Safe, casual topics, she decided gratefully, until he suddenly enquired, 'Do you usually take your holidays alone?'

Instantly she tensed up. That almost criticising note was back in his voice and now that he'd brought the conversation back to a personal level, she had to remind herself to be on her guard.

She thought of Matt Cotton, whom she'd been seeing on a purely platonic level for a year or so before they had parted six months ago. He'd been the only man she had ever considered getting serious with—serious enough to go on holiday with, at any rate. But after their relationship had moved up a notch, the first weekend she had slept with him when they had gone away together, she'd been so disillusioned by his suggestion that they move in together 'to see how it goes' that it had come as quite a shock to her to realise that she wanted more than Matt was offering. What she wanted was the sort of relationship that her parents had enjoyed. A lifelong commitment inspired by love and trust and respect for each other—and she intended to settle for nothing less.

Considering King's question now about taking her holidays alone, and feeling that she was still on the end of a subtle line of interrogation, she enquired pointedly, 'Would you have asked me that if I were a man?'

The arching of an eyebrow as those compellingly blue eyes tugged over her assured her that she was anything but.

'If you were my woman, I wouldn't be happy with you roaming around a strange country on your own.'

'But I'm not your woman, am I?' Bright emeralds fastened on steel as she met his gaze, reminded by the raw sensuality with which he was looking at her of how much she had once longed to be just that. The woman he drove home, undressed and adored in long, exotic nights of pleasure, while she writhed on his bed, allowing his lips and hands licence to every hidden treasure of her body.

Shockingly her breasts burgeoned into life without any warning, their weight heavy and aching, their tips excruciatingly tender against the full cups of her bra.

Surely she didn't still want him in that way? Not now. Not after the way he had supported Mitch in treating her father as he had, when all he had been trying to do was claim what was rightfully his.

'That's right—you're not,' he stated, causing her to flinch from the way he managed to make it sound as though she was the last person he'd ever consider taking to bed. Which was ludicrous! When she would have rejected any overtures from him with every fighting cell in her body! 'And you haven't answered my question—which wasn't intended with any lack of political correctness or offence to your femininity. Do you usually take your holidays alone?'

Fighting off a barrage of conflicting emotions, she shrugged and answered, 'No, not usually. But as I told you last night, my mother's been ill.' Very ill, she appended silently, thinking of the operation and the treatment that Cynthia Hardwicke had had to go through during the past year. 'There hasn't been much time for holidays. But when her old school-friend invited her over to her villa, I realised I was on my knees from all the months of worry and that I was desperate for a holiday too. I'm ashamed to say it, but I think it hit me even harder than it hit Mum,' she found herself admitting to him. 'You can't possibly imagine the unbelievable strain it can put you under when something like that happens to someone you love.'

A dark shadow seemed to cross his features. 'Oh, believe me, I can,' he assured her grimly.

She frowned, and then almost immediately realised. Of course. He was talking about his father.

'What happened to Mitch?' she enquired unnecessarily, because she remembered her parents telling her in the past. But a stranger wouldn't know, would she? Rayne reminded herself. And that was what she was as far as King Clayborne was concerned. A stranger.

'A road accident,' he said, and his words were hard and clipped. 'It deprived him of his mobility—and of his wife.' *Your stepmother,* she nearly said, but didn't. She wasn't supposed to know, was she?

'That's dreadful,' she empathised, because hearing it again—and so many years on—didn't make it any less tragic. She couldn't understand though why he sounded quite so... what? Bitter, she decided.

'What about you?' Putting down his cup, the inscrutable mask was firmly back in place again. 'Have you any brothers or sisters?'

Rayne shook her head.

'And your father?'

'What about him?' she enquired, sounding unintentionally defensive.

'You haven't mentioned him.' The glance he shot her was a little too keen.

Rayne felt tension creep into her jaw. 'He died—just over a year ago.'

'I'm sorry.'

No, you're not, she thought acridly. *But you will be! You and your father! I can promise you that!*

Because she was certain that it was her parents' financial difficulties following her father's bankruptcy, and then the shock of his unexpected death from a heart attack that had made her mother ill. That was when she had vowed to right the wrong that the Claybornes had done to her family. After all Cynthia Hardwicke had been through, though, Rayne didn't want to do anything to worry her. But with her mother having been persuaded to go off to Majorca, Rayne had been able to come away without too many awkward questions being asked.

'So what do you do when you aren't running around this country picking up strange men?'

She ignored the deliberate snipe. 'I type a little.'

'You type?'

'Well, a lot, actually.' Well, she did, didn't she?

'Are you saying you're a PA?'

She chewed on the inside of her mouth, trying not to compound the lies. 'No. I'm freelance.'

'You work for an agency?'

She shook her head. 'For myself.'

'Typing.'

She didn't know why he sounded so disparaging. 'That takes up a fair proportion of my work.' Which was true, she thought. It did. 'What's so strange about that?'

'Only that you strike me as a woman who would have carved out a more determined career path for herself.'

Rayne was glad he couldn't detect how her deception made her heart skip a beat. 'I have.' She saw the question in the heart-stopping clarity of his steel-blue eyes and letting her own slide away, told him trenchantly, 'Seducing rich elderly men!'

His mouth twitched at the corners as though he were trying to assess the authenticity of her remark.

'I think it's time we left,' he stated blandly.

The journey back was an uncomfortable one, not because of King's driving, because he handled the Lamborghini like a dream. But since leaving the café he had barely said two words to her and now, motivated by the view from the ribbon of road that displayed the whole sweep of Monaco below them, Rayne tried to lighten the mood a little by remarking, 'This scenery's unbelievable. So is this weather! Was it as lovely as this in New York?'

'Who said I was in New York?'

Mistake! Rayne admonished herself, feeling those perspicacious eyes roving over her like a hawk's, waiting for her to show any weakness; waiting to pounce.

She shrugged and said as nonchalantly as she could, 'Mitch.' She could hardly tell King that she'd run a check on him before she'd been stupid enough to come here. Because that was how she was beginning to feel, she realised, despairing at herself. Utterly, utterly stupid!

Consoling herself with the thought that she was worrying unnecessarily and that it was only her jumpiness and her overreacting that was creating suspicion in his mind, she ventured to say carelessly, even though it was a lie, 'He led me to believe you were over there on some business or other.'

'Did he now?'

She saw his hands tighten on the wheel, the knuckles whitening above those long dark fingers. But surely Mitch would have known where he was, wouldn't he? She swallowed, her throat suddenly feeling dry.

'Do you come and see him often?'

'Not as often as I should. And I wouldn't be here now if

Hélène hadn't contacted me to tell me Mitch wasn't feeling his best, and also happened to mention the attractive young chauffeuse who had very surprisingly stepped in and taken Talbot's place. I got here as soon as I could, and I'm glad I did.'

'Why? Because you don't trust me?'

'Men in our position can't afford to trust anyone.'

'That's pretty cynical. Is that what money does for you?'

'Unfortunately, yes.'

'So why flaunt it? I mean this car. The Bentley. All those houses you probably own. If you don't want to attract the wrong sort of people you could always drive a Mini.'

'But then I wouldn't be enjoying the benefits of all I worked for.'

All my father worked for! she wanted to scream, and had to bite her tongue to stop the words from tumbling out.

'And is that all you work for?' She couldn't keep the disdain out of her voice as she added pointedly, 'Lamborghinis? Homes in England, Switzerland and who knows where else? Relaxation aboard exclusive yachts?'

'You've really done your homework, haven't you?' He was frowning as he directed a sidelong glance her way, making her realise she had said too much.

'I only know what I read. What everyone reads,' she tagged on quickly, not wanting him to guess how avidly she soaked up any information about him—and always had.

'It isn't just my money that's bothering you, is it, Rayne— if Rayne's even your real name,' he speculated, causing a little shiver to run through her as he operated the remote control switch and opened the gates because they had reached the house. 'It's something much more fundamental than that.'

'Don't be ridiculous! I don't even know you,' she prevaricated with colour suffusing her cheeks as the car growled through the gates towards the exclusive villa standing in its prominent position, high in the hills.

'Maybe not,' he agreed, pulling up outside and cutting the engine, then making every nerve in her body zing as he threw his door open and added with nerve-racking purpose, 'But I think the time has come to change all that.'

CHAPTER THREE

'YOU'VE got it all wrong!' Rayne threw over her shoulder, flying ahead of him into the villa. Her blood was pounding in her ears, her racing heart making her sound as though she'd just run five miles.

'Have I?' King demanded grimly, the strength of his own hormones putting a flush across his high cheekbones. 'I'm not a callow youth, Rayne, and if your story holds any water—as I'd like to believe it does—I can't think of any other reason why you constantly feel the need to antagonise me.'

Oh, dear heaven...! She stopped dead, breathing hard, her lashes coming down over her eyes, because he could see it, even though she was refusing to. But how could it be this strong, she wondered hopelessly, when she despised him as much as she despised Mitchell Clayborne? It was as if all of her pent-up teenage frustrations about him had rushed back and were screaming to be dealt with. But how could he be so astute? How could he tell?

Dry-mouthed, she touched her tongue to her top lip as he turned her round to face him.

'You terrify me,' she said, startling herself, because surely that was Lorri speaking. The hapless kid who had adored him from a distance, and who would have died for him, given half the chance. Not the mature twenty-five-year-old who knew him for what he was and hated him with every trembling bone in her body.

'I know,' he acknowledged sagaciously. 'But it's yourself you're afraid of, Rayne. The fear of an involvement that wasn't in your plans. Well, believe me, my beautiful girl, the thought of what you've been doing to me since I got here—and what you can still do to me—terrifies me, too.'

She laughed, but her throat felt clogged. 'You? Terrified?'

'Does that seem so strange?'

'No, just inconceivable,' she responded, wishing her credit cards were sorted so she could tell him where to go and just get the hell out of there. As it was, she felt like a butterfly caught in a fly-trap whose promise of the sweetest pleasure only hid danger beneath. Her head was spinning and her legs felt weak, while every organ in between was throbbing with the almost uncontrollable need to reach for him, pull him down to her and drown beneath the pleasure of his ravaging mouth, breathe in his heady, far too tantalizing cologne.

'Why? Because I'm a man? And obviously a very experienced one at that?'

'Something like that.' She didn't know what she was saying any more. Couldn't seem to tell him where to go, or drag herself away from him—even if she'd wanted to. Because that was just it, she realised suddenly. She didn't.

'I might be a man of the world, but I'm willing to bet you could give me a run for my money.'

Was that what he thought? Rayne swallowed, guessing that he would probably laugh if she told him how few sexual encounters she had had in her lifetime.

'And that's your experience speaking, of course.'

'Of course.'

Well, that's where you're wrong! she wanted to fling at him, wishing she had the nerve to play along with him and do what some other women in her position might do. Flatter his ego and enjoy a brief spell of the pleasure he could give her, then watch his anger explode when he found out who she really was and realised she'd made a fool of him. Oh, to hurt him as he'd hurt her! Hurt her father when he'd joined Mitch in taking what had never been theirs to take! But common sense warned her that men of King Clayborne's character couldn't be hurt, and that even to entertain such a tempting idea was no less than crazy.

Instead she said, 'Well, dream on, King. I didn't come here to have a fling with you or anybody else, and you're very much mistaken if you think I did!'

'Not intentionally, no.'

Pulling herself out of his disturbing sphere, she viewed him warily from under her lashes. 'And what's that supposed to mean?' she challenged shakily.

'I'm sure you didn't intend to charm your way in here only to find yourself fighting an attraction that is bigger than you are. Bigger than both of us, if I'm honest. But you're giving off pheromones, Rayne, that no man this side of ninety could possibly ignore. And quite simply, darling, I wouldn't dream of insulting you by pretending to ignore them. And if you refuse to accept the effect you're having on me, I'm sure you're way too experienced not to acknowledge this.'

It was inevitable what was going to happen. But even that acknowledgement couldn't have prepared her for the onslaught on her senses when his head dipped and his hard masculine mouth finally covered hers.

It was like two universes colliding. A barrage of riotous emotions and sensations that rocked her to the very core of her femininity, driving everything from her mind but the need to be kissed and stroked and caressed by this man and this man alone—because she still wanted him, much, much more than she had ever wanted him before, and with a hunger that excited and thrilled her even as it appalled.

And he wanted her too…

She didn't have to be experienced to recognise the rock-hard evidence of just how much as his arm tightened around her, locking her to him, and shamelessly she realised that that was what he had been referring to a moment ago, rather than just the inevitable joining of their hungry, ravenous mouths.

With a small murmur, which was half-need, half-despair, she wound her arms around his neck, glorying in the sensations that his six-feet-plus of power-packed masculinity sent coursing through her as she moved convulsively against his hard warmth.

'Can you deny it now, Rayne?' His voice was hoarse, a ragged whisper against the softness of her cheek. 'What is there to lose in admitting that you want me every bit as much as you've made me want you?'

And just how much he hadn't even realised until now. He'd had women in his time who'd given him pleasure and to whom he'd given pleasure in return. But that was all it had been. Pleasure. This girl, however, had a way about her that excited him and made his anatomy harden to such an extent that it hurt.

But why? Why, when to seduce her had been a cold, calculated plan? When he'd intended to remain detached and—if he was honest with himself—to have her begging, virtually down on her knees, for him to take her?

Well, that just showed him, he thought, mocking himself for his lack of immunity, his inability to stay unaffected, when all he wanted to do right now was rip off her clothes and carry her up to the nearest bed and feel her warm softness closing in around him, her body bucking beneath his as he drove into her.

Steady on, King...

He was breathing raggedly as he lifted his head.

'So what's it to be, Rayne? Your bed or mine?' He was amazed at how cool—how indifferent—he managed to sound.

There was nothing cool, though, or indifferent, about the hand that was suddenly making contact with his left cheek, taking him so unawares he nearly overbalanced.

'How dare you!' Rayne found she was trembling so much

she could hardly get her words out, realising that it wasn't just his effrontery that was responsible for her impulsive action. It was also aggravated by the knowledge that she had invited what had happened between them every inch of the way, so that her anger was directed more at herself and her abandoned response to his kiss rather than at him.

'I'm sorry. I could hardly help jumping to what I believed was a very natural conclusion,' King expressed, holding his smarting cheek, deciding that he had rather overstepped the mark. Nevertheless that still didn't stop him from enquiring mockingly, 'Are you usually prone to bursts of violence?'

'You drove me to it!' It was a small wild cry, born of her despair over responding to him in the way she had, and for striking him, which she was thoroughly ashamed of now.

'You drove yourself to it,' he said quietly. 'Firstly by refusing to acknowledge that there's definitely something between us, and then in not doing so, suddenly finding yourself way out of your depth.' His mouth moved in a kind of contemplative half-smile. 'I'll just put it down to frustration, shall I?' he remarked, his eyes skimming over her in a shaming reminder of what had just transpired.

'Put it down to whatever you like!' she breathed, shocked by the passions he could arouse in her and, pivoting away from him, she fled up the stairs, wanting only to crawl into a hole and pretend that none of her shameless behaviour had ever happened.

In the privacy of her room she sank down on the sumptuous bed, dropped her head into her hands and groaned.

Whatever had come over her? Not only to throw herself at him as she had when he had had the audacity to kiss her, but then to slap him like that afterwards as though it had all been his fault. Being quite honest with herself, she was forced to admit that he was right. She *had* wanted him to kiss her. Wanted it like she had never wanted anything. A man who had hurt her father and, with Mitch, had as good as destroyed her family. Was that why she had hit him? Was it all part of the need for retribution? Or was King Clayborne simply always destined to bring out the worst in her?

Angry tears burned her eyes, but they were tears of remorse and scorching shame too. How could she have responded to him so easily, and without so much as a conscience? Without any thought for what the Claybornes had cost her parents. Was she really that weak? She padded over to the en suite bathroom to try and scrub the taste of King Clayborne off her mouth, promising herself, as well as both of her parents, that she would never let it happen again.

And if he did find out that she had been lying to him?

She shuddered, closing her mind against that intimidating scenario. That was something she definitely refused to think about on top of everything else.

The florist at the other end of the line seemed to be taking forever to deal with the order Rayne was trying to telephone through.

'And the name on the card?' she asked mechanically, in heavily accented English.

'I explained to the lady I spoke to first that I haven't got a card, but she said it would be all right if I brought the cash down before you close this afternoon. My name's Lorrayne Hardwicke,' Rayne told her, sending anxious glances towards the closed door.

She had come in here to the study to make a couple of calls and to try and sort out a birthday bouquet to be sent to her mother. She'd wanted to do it from the privacy of her own suite, but the maids were changing the bed and giving the rooms an extra fine clean today, and time was getting scarce if she wanted her mother to receive her flowers in the morning.

'I'm afraid I cannot process the order unless we receive the credit or the money…what is it you say? Upfront,' the woman emphasised, remembering. 'I'm sorry, *mademoiselle*, but those are the conditions.'

'But your manageress distinctly assured me it would be all right,' Rayne despaired. She hadn't missed sending her mother flowers on her birthday since she was eighteen, when things had started really going downhill for her parents. And OK, she couldn't pay with a card, but she had a small amount of cash that she had earned from chauffeuring Mitch around, and the florist *had* said it would be all right.

'My manageress has just left for the afternoon. I will try and get hold of her and ring you back if you will give me your number. What did you say your name was?'

'Lorrayne Hardwicke.'

'Can you spell that, please?'

Rayne darted another glance towards the door as she heard voices on the other side of it.

'I'll call you back,' she said quickly, snapping her cellphone shut a fraction of a second before the door opened and King walked in.

'What the…?' His smile for whomever he had been talking to outside was wiped away by surprise at seeing her sitting there behind his father's desk.

'My room's being cleaned and I needed to make a couple of calls,' she told him croakily, not sure what was disturbing her most. Nearly being caught red-handed blurting out who she really was, or the visual images of what had happened between them earlier in the day. 'Of course, if I'm intruding…' She was already swivelling back on the studded leather chair.

'I wouldn't say that.'

In fact he was looking at her over what seemed like an acre of polished mahogany as though he was imagining her naked and spreadeagled across it. Or was that just what her own wild imaginings were conjuring up? She slammed the lid down on her errant thoughts before they could manifest themselves on her face. 'I…I didn't hear you come in.'

'Evidently not.' He'd been to pick up Mitch at his own insistence, and had come in here to find his pen to sign some letters his secretary had faxed through while he was gone. 'Otherwise you wouldn't be acting as though I'd just caught you rifling through the silver cabinets.' A distracted smile twisted the sensuous line of his lower lip. 'Perhaps that's it,' he declared airily, pocketing his pen. 'Are you looking for something, Rayne?'

'No.' At least that much was true. If she had been, it would be for the evidence that would prove that MiracleMed was her father's. She knew, though, that she didn't have a cat in hell's chance of finding it here in this luxurious Mediterranean retreat, if in fact any proof existed at all.

'If you must know, I'm just a bit peeved because I was trying to order some flowers for Mum,' she told him, gripping the padded arms of the chair, which she seemed to have become rooted to ever since he had come in, 'but it seems you can't even breathe these days if you haven't got a credit card.'

He nodded. 'Make the call,' he advised. To her stunned surprise, he was taking his wallet from the inside pocket of his jacket. 'Make the call,' he reiterated, taking out a credit card.

'I...I couldn't possibly,' she stammered, blushing to her roots as she realised how her statement must have sounded. As though she was asking him to help her. 'I didn't mean I wanted you to...'

'What's the number?' he asked, ignoring her embarrassment.

Seeing how determined he was, she quoted it from the piece of paper she'd jotted it down on earlier.

'Now what is it you want?'

With a little shrug, feeling indebted, uncertainly she told him. He dealt with it swiftly and effortlessly. And not only that—in fluent French!

'And the recipient?' he enquired, reverting to English to ask her.

Cynthia Hardwicke, she almost said, realising only just in time that that would blow her cover good and proper. 'Address it to "Mum," care of...' Casually she filled him in with the name of the friend her mother was staying with. 'And the message is simply, *Happy Birthday. Love from Rayne.'*

It took him just seconds, it seemed, to supply the florist with his own details, his voice deep and confident, its dark rich timbre sending an unwanted tingle along Rayne's spine.

'Thanks,' she murmured when he had finished, unable to look at him as she came around the desk. 'I really wasn't asking you to do that. I can let you have the cash.'

'There's no hurry,' he said, his tone surprisingly reassuring, the sudden touch of his hand on her shoulder bringing her startled gaze to his.

She looked instantly wary, King thought, noticing the guarded emotion in the green-gold depths of her eyes. They were, quite simply, the most beautiful eyes he had seen on any woman he'd ever met, but there was some other emotion behind the wariness that was defying him to touch her. Sadness, he was startled to recognise. Deep-buried, but not altogether concealed. And he knew in that moment that somehow—somewhere—those eyes had penetrated his consciousness before. Last week? Last year? He gave a mental shrug. Perhaps it was only in his dreams.

'We got off to a bad start.' He was surprised at how hoarse his voice sounded. Was it because his hormones had kicked in again, causing him to harden from the warmth of her body through her thin blouse? Or was it the dark and heady mixture of her perfume? 'I thought it might be sensible if we were both to try again.' Otherwise she'd get away from him, he was sure, and he'd never lost a woman he'd set his heart on having in his life.

'Try?' she ventured croakily, realising why she had never stood a chance against his potent masculinity as a teenager. He was really quite amazing. With those dynamically dark looks. In the way he spoke. The way he carried himself. As if he owned the world. Which he probably did. Or a fair proportion of it anyway, she thought cynically, resenting him for how rich he was, how influential, and for making her wish that she was spreadeagled over that desk with him...

'To be civil to each other,' she heard him saying. 'I'll accept that your reason for being here is all above board. And you...' He was massaging his lower jaw with his free hand. 'You'll promise to keep your hands to yourself.'

Wings of colour touched her cheeks from his all too shaming reminder of how she had struck him. 'As long as you promise to do the same with yours.'

'If that's what you want.'

Rayne felt her throat constrict. 'What's that supposed to mean?'

He smiled silkily. 'You know very well.'

Yes, she did. The last thing she wanted was for him to spell it out, but it seemed he was going to anyway as he went on.

'Calling a truce, unfortunately, isn't going to put paid to the fact that there's a definite chemistry between us, Rayne, even if you do want to deny it. But a woman doesn't respond to a man the way you responded to me unless she wants that man to make love to her. Even if she is, as I'd very much like to rule out, a woman with some other agenda.'

'I got carried away—that was all,' she said quickly, hating to admit it but desperate to quash any adverse notion in his mind about her reasons for being there. 'So. I find you attractive.' Who wouldn't? 'But we don't always give in to what our baser instincts are telling us to do, do we? I'm sorry I reacted in the way I did.' She was referring to striking him. 'I was just a bit wound up, that's all. Unprepared...'

'For what happened between us?'

She nodded.

'And are you still unprepared?'

No, she wasn't, she realised, because even this conversation with him was turning her on, making her body zing with a host of traitorous impulses.

'I can deal with it,' she said huskily, wishing she could tear herself away from him, but she couldn't seem to do it.

'Can you?' When she didn't respond, too sensually aware to answer, coolly he suggested, 'Let's see.'

As he was speaking he'd positioned himself on the edge of the desk. Now, as his arm snaked around her tiny waist, Rayne lost her balance and shot out a hand to steady herself, gasping as she made unwitting contact with the hard, bunching muscles of his thigh.

The intimacy sent shock waves coursing through her body. She could tell from King's sharply drawn breath that it was having a devastating effect on him too.

'Heaven help me if you weren't sent here just to drive me out of my mind!' he rasped before his mouth came down to plunder the warm, willing cavern of hers.

This time she didn't stop to think because the scent and sound and feel of him were driving her insane for him and suddenly she was utterly lost to the eager and hungry demands of her own body.

When he tugged her blouse open and pulled a lacy cup down over her full, high breast, she arched her back, angling her body in sweet invitation to him to take the hard throbbing tip into his mouth.

Proud of her femininity, she writhed between his thighs, thrilling in his strength as he used them to clamp her to him, while he continued to drive her crazy by suckling harder at her breast.

Unlocking her womb, she thought crazily, as sensations spiralled downwards to the most secret heart of her, making her hot and moist in readiness for the hard penetration of his body.

'Deny it all you like, you're going to be my woman, Rayne. You *are* my woman. Understand?' he breathed raggedly against the sensitised hollow of her ear. 'Otherwise why would you let me do this?' His fingers found her other breast, making her gasp and strain against him as he tormented the sensitive bud. 'Or this?' His other hand slid down her body to clasp her buttock, caressing and moulding, its heat searing through her thin trousers before it moved possessively round to cup her aching femininity. 'Why?' he demanded huskily. 'If you can't accept that, too?'

She wanted to protest. She knew she should. But how could she? she demanded chaotically of herself. When she knew she had been made for this! That she was his and always had been, and that even if her mind recognised the treachery of acknowledging it, her body wouldn't listen.

But she had to make it listen…

He's your enemy. So what does that make you?

Dredging up every ounce of self-discipline that she could muster, she wrenched herself away from him.

'I don't want this!' she choked, dragging the back of her hand across her mouth.

'Really?' Still perched on the edge of the desk, he was breathing as heavily as she was. 'Then you're putting up a darn good show of convincing me otherwise.'

'I don't care what you think.' Which was a joke, she thought distractedly, even as she said it. Because, for some strange reason she still did. 'I don't want to get involved with you.'

'Why not? When it's so patently obvious that we could be good together?' He looked hot and flushed and still so obviously aroused. 'Are you in a relationship with someone else?'

'That's none of your business,' she snapped, straightening her clothes with faltering fingers.

'So you aren't,' he deduced correctly.

Because wouldn't it have been the best way of keeping him at bay, she thought, realising it too late, if she had said she was?

'So what was it, Rayne? A disappointing attachment?'

You could say that! her heart screamed bitterly, because there had been nothing that had shamed or disillusioned her more than her reckless crush on him.

'I just don't go in for casual sleeping around.'

'I'm pleased to hear it,' he responded deeply, his eyes fixing on her with a dark intensity. She looked really quite shaken, he thought, wondering why, when in every other way she seemed so much a woman of the world. 'For what it's worth…it doesn't rank very highly with me, either.'

'Hah!' Despite her brittle little laugh, she couldn't help wondering if he was telling the truth. She wanted to kick herself for hoping that he was.

'You really have a very low opinion of me, don't you?' he remarked, running a long tapered hand through his thick hair. She was surprised to notice that it was trembling slightly.

So even the high-and-mighty Kingsley Clayborne was human!

She wondered why she was even allowing herself to grant him any concessions, and put it down to the fact that she was so affected by him—by what she had allowed him to do to her—that she was still too unsettled by it to feel anything.

'Why should it matter to you what I—' she began as she was smoothing back her hair, but broke off when a stick prodding the door he'd failed to close brought it flying open. Both of them had been too otherwise preoccupied to hear the wheelchair approaching.

'King? Rayne? Oh, there you both are!' Mitchell Clayborne's colour was unusually high as he manoeuvred his chair into the room and Rayne guessed he'd been doing too much, against his doctor's orders.

'King, I wanted you to retrieve the book I dropped down behind the bedside cabinet but, since Rayne's here, she can do it for me and perhaps read a little to me. Have you finished with her?'

King's eyes were speculative as, on his feet now, he regarded her from his superior height, looking totally unfazed by what had just happened between them.

'Yes, I've finished with her,' he told his father.

Reluctantly inhaling his scent, keen to get away, Rayne brushed past him, although she could tell from that slight compression of his devastating mouth that what he was really saying was that where she was concerned he hadn't even begun yet.

CHAPTER FOUR

THE following day Rayne decided to escape from the house for a while, needing some time to decide what she was going to do.

She was uncomfortable associating with the people who had wreaked such devastation on her family, but she couldn't see what else she could do. She didn't want to leave there without the evidence or admission that she was determined to secure for her father's sake.

She had started asking Mitch questions last night while she had been reading to him—very subtly, and supposedly innocently. Like how he had begun in business. And when exactly had he hit upon the idea for the MiracleMed software. How he had felt when it had taken off.

'King must have been very proud of you,' she'd ventured, assessing his reaction, looking for any change in his hard, world-weary features, any note of guilt in his gravelly voice.

He'd seemed all right at first. But then he'd grown more and more agitated, even when their conversation had reverted to more casual topics. As well he should have! Rayne thought bitterly.

He'd looked so unwell, though, and had sounded so breathless that her conscience wouldn't allow her to ask any more leading questions.

'I think you should go to bed,' she had advised worriedly, ringing the bell to summon one of the male members of staff to help him. She was frustrated, though, that yet another day had gone by and she was still no nearer to realising her goal.

Now, this morning, he had sent for her and told her that he didn't need her services today, and so she'd decided to take herself down into the town for a proper look around.

'You'll need some of these,' he'd told her from his bed, pressing a whole wad of banknotes into her hand.

Shocked and embarrassed, she had thrust them back at him. 'I can't,' she'd protested, appalled at taking money from anyone—let alone someone she despised so much.

'Don't be silly. How do you think you're going to get around and buy the odd souvenir?' he'd demanded of her gruffly. 'With those big bright eyes and that naturally winning smile?'

Shrugging off his compliment, she had to accept that he was right. Being robbed hadn't exactly left her in a position to be proud.

'I'll pay you back,' she'd promised resolutely, not only for his benefit, but for her own. She didn't like being in this man's debt any more than she wanted to like him, but he was making it very hard for her not to do either.

Now, coming down into the hall, her heart sank when King appeared, looking dynamic in dark blue corduroys and an ivory-white shirt that left his forearms bare, just as she was asking one of the maids in her somewhat limited French if she could call her a cab.

One fluent instruction from him in the girl's own language had the young maid almost bobbing in compliance before she cast a swift glance at Rayne and darted away.

'What did you say to her?' Rayne enquired, puzzled, because it certainly didn't sound like anything as simple as ordering a taxi.

'I told her I'd take care of it,' he replied succinctly and without any of the mental disturbance that just the sight of him was producing in her.

'I don't need you to rescue me from every difficult situation,' she assured him with a slight tremor marking her words, unintentionally conveying to him how unsettled he was making her feel.

'Nevertheless…you've got me.' There was triumph in the clear blue eyes that drifted lazily over her tie-waisted chequered blouse and white cut-offs. 'Now, where did you want to go?'

'Nowhere in particular,' she said, being deliberately obstructive. She wanted his help even less than she wanted his father's, and she certainly didn't welcome how her body was responding just from the way he was looking at her. 'I was just going to do a bit of sightseeing—and without having to worry about the car,' she told him, wishing he'd just take out his phone and order the cab he'd said he'd deal with.

But with a hand at her elbow, sending her thoughts spinning into chaos, he said, 'In that case, I'll be more than delighted to show you around.'

She wanted to protest. To tell him that she was going out because the strain was proving too much, being in this house with her father's bitterest enemies and not feeling able to tell them who she was. But mainly, she decided, it was because of King himself. Because he disturbed her equilibrium so much and made her feel so ashamed of how he made her feel every time he came near her that she wanted to put as much distance between him and herself as she possibly could.

But with King Clayborne, she was discovering, argument was futile.

Consequently, it was with a raging awareness of him and a mind that was far from relaxed that she allowed him to drive her into town.

She was relieved, though, when he kept the conversation light. Impersonal. Not touching on any awkward topics. Like why he made rockets go off inside her every time he touched her. Or why she pretended not to want to go to bed with him, when every betraying cell in her body assured him that she did!

Instead, he acquainted her with the lesser-known facts about Monaco as they drove down through its flower-decked streets which, earlier in the season, formed the circuit for the world-famous motor racing Grand Prix. And he gave her an insight into the country's history and its royalty, making it interesting for her. Making her want to know more as she listened to his deep and sensually caressing voice, remembering how it had warmed and excited her all those years ago.

'Did your mother receive the flowers?' he asked as he finished parking the Lamborghini in a space he had had no difficulty finding.

'Yes, thank you,' Rayne responded succinctly.

'Did she like them?'

'Probably,' she answered minimally again.

She caught the curiosity in his eyes and in the faint smile that touched his hard yet exciting mouth, and she knew she had to explain. He had paid for them, after all.

'When I rang Mum earlier, the friend she's staying with said she was still asleep. She offered to wake her to show them to her, but I thought it best not to disturb her. After what she's been through, she needs to get all the rest and relaxation she can.'

'She must appreciate having such a thoughtful and caring daughter,' he commented, taking the keys out of the ignition.

'She deserves no less,' Rayne expressed, absurdly warmed by what had been no less than a compliment from him. 'She's always been there for me.'

'You've been fortunate in having such a good relationship with your mother.'

'Didn't you with your mother?'

The question slipped out and she didn't know why she had asked it. He could have had seven doting mothers for all it meant to her.

'My parents divorced when I was five. My father got custody. I only saw my mother on a few occasions after that. She preferred rearing horses to rearing children. The last I heard, she was living on a stud farm with her third husband somewhere in Colorado.'

Rayne shrugged. 'That's a pity,' she said, meaning it.

In answer she saw the firm masculine mouth compress. 'Not really. I went to boarding school, which was best for Mitch and for me. I learned how to be self-sufficient—independent—from a very early age, which stood me in good stead, as it turned out.' He wasn't actually spelling it out, but Rayne didn't need to ask to know that he was talking about Mitch's accident. 'I don't know whether I would have been so equipped to handle everything that was thrust on me if I'd had the type of family life that most people take for granted. I think it's true what they say. That what you've never had, you never miss.'

Rayne didn't wholly agree with that. After all, if he had had a bit more maternal love perhaps he wouldn't have been so ruthless and insensitive towards other people. Like her father, she thought achingly, her teeth clamping together as she looked away.

'I was lucky,' she murmured half to herself and in a tone that emphasised the whole poignancy of her loss. 'Dad was always there too and he was quite simply the most caring, understanding and honourable man I've ever met.'

'Quite a happy family, then?' He sounded quite cynical, and Rayne wondered why. Was it because he hadn't known that sort of stability himself? Being packed off to boarding school. Being made to feel abandoned—although he hadn't said so—by both his parents.

She could almost have felt sorry for him, except that King Clayborne wasn't the type of man to inspire pity.

Even so, against all the odds, she was surprised to find herself enjoying his company as he guided her around the

Principality. She even found herself laughing at something he was saying as he brought her across the tree-fringed square that gave onto the wide imposing frontage of the palace.

Pale and majestic with its crenellated towers, it was once the home, Rayne reminded herself, of the beautiful actress of the nineteen-fifties who had been plucked out of Hollywood and brought here by her prince, only to steal the hearts of his people.

In fact there were photographs of her adorning shop windows all over the town, Rayne had noticed, still a lure for the tourists even so many years after her death, a beautiful legend whose name had become synonymous with Monaco.

'It must have been like a fairy tale for her,' Rayne whispered a little later when she saw yet another image of the princess in the latest shop window they were passing. 'To win not only a prince's love—but a whole country's.'

'Even a country that is less than five hundred acres across.'

She pulled a face and smiled, amazed at how small an area Monaco took up, amazed too by King's knowledge of it.

'And you? Do you believe in fairy tales, Rayne?' he asked, his voice suddenly strung with mocking amusement.

'Fairy tales?' She pretended to be considering it as she looked up at him askance.

'Happy ever afters. Two people living side by side and loving each other until death they do part.'

'Well, it's obvious you don't,' she lobbed back, noting the cynicism with which he'd said it. But then, after the way his parents' marriage had broken up, she supposed she could understand why.

'I know what Mum and Dad had,' she murmured almost reverently. 'All right, it wasn't exactly a fairy tale. They had their ups and downs. But they loved each other, and knew they always would.' And they had instilled in their only daughter the importance of the qualities that kept a marriage strong. Love, trust and faithfulness. It was something she strongly believed in and it was something she staunchly refused to allow anyone to dismiss lightly. Even King Clayborne. 'You were just unlucky,' she said, moving away from the window and the image that had sparked off this unwelcome conversation with him in the first place.

The cathedral. The palace. The exotic gardens. They did it all. He even showed her the amazingly palatial building of the famous casino, although they didn't actually go inside.

It wasn't until they got back into the car that Rayne realised she'd switched her phone off before going into the cathedral and had forgotten to switch it back on. She chastened herself for letting everything go out of her mind simply because she was with King.

She started when her phone began to ring almost as soon as she had switched it on.

'Lorrayne?' Cynthia Hardwicke said when Rayne put the phone to her ear.

Immediately Rayne tensed up. King hadn't yet switched the car's engine on. Could he have heard the way her mother had addressed her?

Trying to sound normal, she wished her mother a happy birthday when she had finished enthusing about the bouquet Rayne had sent her.

'I'm glad you like it,' she breathed, relaxing a little, relieved to hear her mother sounding so buoyant. She envisaged Cynthia Hardwicke, with her grey-tinged auburn hair freshly tinted for her holiday, starting to regain the weight she had lost, her skin—usually as pale as her own—beginning to bloom again beneath a welcome Majorcan sun.

'Like them? I can't tell you how much they've brightened my day! But why did you have the message signed "Rayne", love?' She gave a little chuckle. 'Weren't you thinking?'

Catching her breath, Rayne cast a surreptitious glance at King.

He was scanning through various menus on his own phone.

Checking appointments and deleting texts, she decided, her eyes drawn to that strong, steady hand that had driven her nearly mindless for him yesterday.

He still hadn't started the engine, letting her take her call.

Killing time, she suspected, while he waited for her to finish. Nevertheless, she knew that although he was displaying all outward signs of being courteous and respecting her privacy by appearing otherwise engaged, that sharp brain of his was probably attuned to every agitated response she was uttering.

'I couldn't have been. I'm sorry,' she added quickly, because she certainly didn't feel happy being forced to deceive her own mother. 'But you're all right, are you?' she asked uneasily, having sensed a flicker of interest from the man beside her since uttering that apology, even though he still appeared preoccupied with the obvious running of his business.

'Of course I am,' Cynthia Hardwicke assured her, although there was a curious note in the disembodied voice. 'But are you? You don't sound yourself, darling. Is anything the matter?'

'No, of course not.' She laughed to try and convince her parent that everything was as it should be, to try and behave normally.

'Are you with someone?'

Rayne could feel herself growing hot and sticky from her toes upwards.

'Who is it?' Her mother persisted in wanting to know.

Rayne hesitated before replying. 'It's just a friend.' Involuntarily, her gaze strayed to King and his heart-stopping profile. It exhibited forcefulness overlaid with unstinting sensuality. Authority and energy, harnessed with a magnetism that had the drawing power over a woman that the moon had over the tides. But he had obviously picked up the gist of the conversation because his mouth was twitching now in what she could only describe as sensual mockery. He clearly didn't regard her as a friend, any more than she considered him one. Though for plainly different reasons where she was concerned!

'I thought I knew all your friends,' Cynthia pressed. Which was true, Rayne thought. She did. 'You're sounding pretty secretive. That's not like you.'

'It's no one of any significance,' Rayne stressed, already regretting the comment when she saw the way King was looking at her as she wound up the conversation and rang off.

'Why didn't you tell her about us?' he enquired, turning all his attention towards her now.

'There is no "us",' she reminded him tartly, feeling the heat of shame creeping up her neck and into her cheeks when a masculine eyebrow lifted in obvious dispute.

'No? Not when I only have to touch you to send your hormones rocketing through the roof? I'd say that was significant enough to constitute an "us".'

He'd also taken her out to breakfast that first morning. Showed her around Monte Carlo and bought her lunch today. Not to mention making his credit card available to pay for her mother's birthday bouquet!

'I'm sorry about the way I described you,' she felt she had to offer, even if his reasons for helping her might be purely self-motivated. 'But I had to put her off the scent.'

'The scent of what?' he asked smoothly.

'That I'm here.'

'In Monaco? Or with me?'

'Both,' she answered truthfully now. 'She thinks I'm staying with my friend in Nice. If I told her I was in Monte Carlo on my own, she'd worry.'

'And if you said you were with me?'

'Then I'd have to explain how I came to be in Mitch's house in the first place, and she'd worry even more.' No, more than that. She'd have a fit, Rayne thought, shuddering to think what Cynthia Hardwicke would say if she knew that her daughter was hobnobbing with the family who had ruined her husband. Another shiver went down her spine as she thought of how easily she could become involved—especially with King—if she didn't watch her step.

'You don't think she'd approve of you picking up older men?'

'I didn't pick him up,' she reminded him, stressing the point. 'I meant I'd have to tell her how I'd had my belongings stolen. With losing Dad so recently, Mum gets worked up about things and imagines something terrible's going to happen to me. If she thought I needed her in any way, she'd be over here like a shot, and I couldn't risk letting her do that.' Even if the Claybornes hadn't been in the picture. 'She needs her holiday a hundred times more than I need mine. I don't intend doing anything that would spoil it for her.'

'That's very commendable,' he murmured, the sound rumbling deeply from his chest. 'You love her very much, don't you?'

His observation was, like his eyes, so direct and probing that she looked quickly away without answering, ashamed to let such a hard-headed character as he was see the welling emotion she had to fight to control.

King couldn't take his eyes off her tight, tense features— the perfect structure of her forehead, the pert nose with those slightly flaring nostrils, the gentle curve of her cheek.

This girl was a real enigma, he decided, with his face a study in concentration. On the one hand she seemed guarded and extremely defensive, which aroused his natural suspicions, especially since he'd taken her as a gold-digger. Definitely like someone with something to hide. Yet on the other hand she spoke about and behaved towards her mother as though she would give her life for the woman if she had to, which didn't quite tie in with the hard-headed opportunist he was prepared to think she was. He was finding, he realised, that he harboured very conflicting opinions about

Rayne Carpenter, and it wasn't in his nature to be confounded by anyone. And on top of that there was still this strong and nagging feeling of having known her before...

'We all do things according to what our consciences tell us we should do, don't we?' she suggested meaningfully, wishing she could control her tongue and not let her emotions run away with her until she was ready to hit him—and his father—with the truth.

'Should it prick my conscience that every time you come within a yard of me I want to take you to bed?' he said softly, fondling her hair. 'Or that you want me to against your own better judgement?'

The space between them was suddenly charged with so much electricity it was as if someone had lit a whole boxful of fire-crackers and Rayne's heart started hammering in her chest.

'Can we drop this subject? Please,' she breathed emphatically.

Her breath seemed to stick in her lungs as his arm came across the back of her seat, bringing him closer to her.

'Have you never heard the expression "He who pleads is lost"?' he murmured with his smile predatory, his lashes thick and dark, shielding his eyes as they rested on the fullness of her trembling, slightly parted mouth.

When his lips touched hers it was only to make contact with the outer corner of her mouth, a contact that left her craving the full onslaught of his kiss, made her grasp the seat to stop herself from twining her arms around his warm, muscled torso as he lifted his head.

'What's wrong, Rayne? Can't you accept the consequences of what you've got yourself into?' His voice was quite steady, not ragged with sexual desire as she'd imagined it would be. In fact there was a note of hidden danger in the very choice of his words.

'I wasn't aware I'd got myself into anything,' she uttered

tremulously, knowing he was still suspicious of her, still vigilant, even if she had imagined that softening in him just now, because she had, she realised, telling herself now that she had been a fool to do so.

'Then you obviously need convincing,' he said.

She expected him to demonstrate exactly what he meant, but he didn't. Instead he simply started the powerful car and drove them back to the villa.

So what had he meant by that? she wondered when, once there, he left her to her own devices, abandoning her to deal with some business in the study. Did he intend to keep her on tenterhooks—make her wait until her guard was down before proving his point to her again? That she couldn't resist him. Or had he guessed the secret she was keeping from him and Mitch and was merely luring her into a false sense of security until such time as he disclosed what he had uncovered?

And that was a very unfortunate pun, Rayne decided with a grimace because, if she wasn't careful, she was in danger of him not only guessing who she really was before she was ready to tell him, but also of winding up in his bed! And wouldn't that be a double victory for him? She shivered just from the thought of it, although even self-loathing couldn't temper the excitement that heated her blood every time she considered him being her lover.

'I don't think you should be doing this,' Rayne counselled, watching Mitch manoeuvring his chair along the wooded path where he had insisted she bring him today. 'Getting out so early so as to give everyone the slip is one thing, but persuading me to bring you over such uneven ground as this—'

'Will you shut up?' Mitch said, carrying on ahead of her, his hard mottled hands on the wheels pushing him stubbornly to his goal.

The trees thinned out, making Rayne gasp, not only from the sheer danger of the cliff edge just below them, but at the panorama of nothing but glittering sea and sky that had suddenly opened up in front of them.

'Can you show me anything better than that?' Mitch challenged, waving a hand towards the view. 'I used to come here a lot when I was young. It's where I proposed to my first wife.'

'King's mother,' Rayne said tentatively.

'Did you know she left me?' He gave a harsh bark of laughter. 'Of course you did. Everybody knows it. Everyone knows I'm not the easiest of men to live with.'

Rayne glanced down at him, noting something that sounded remarkably like regret in his voice. Did he still miss the woman who had deserted him and their five-year-old child? Miss her still, even though he'd finally found someone else to take her place?

'As a boy, King blamed himself for his mother leaving us. For leaving him,' Mitch was saying, much to Rayne's surprise. 'It hardened him. Made a cynic of him. Especially where marriage and family is concerned. We never could form the bond we should have formed. He was already a man by the time I met Karen.'

'Your second wife?' A woman half his age, who had died so tragically when their car had come off the road, Rayne reflected, although it was King she was reluctantly thinking of. King, the child who had lost a mother, even though she was still alive. And King the man, who was left scarred by the desertion. Left hard and uncaring. Unable to trust...

Mitch nodded and started to cough. 'Here. Help me with this thing, will you?' he spluttered.

He was having difficulty opening the zip of a leather pouch he'd brought with him. When she gave it back to him, he swore when he looked inside.

'What's wrong?' Rayne asked him anxiously.

'Does anything have to be wrong?' he wheezed, turning his chair with such angry force that it lurched sideways, lodging one wheel in a grassy hollow.

Rayne shot over to grab the handles, trying to pull it free.

'I can't move it!' she gasped, finding the man's bulk and the awkward angle of the chair too much for her inadequate strength. To add to that, Mitch's breathing was beginning to worry her.

'I'm going to ring King,' she said quickly, taking out her phone when her attempts to dislodge the chair proved ineffectual.

'No! We don't need him,' Mitch protested to her dismay.

'I'll have to,' Rayne told him, too frightened by the danger of the situation to be intimidated by him, even if every bone in her body rebelled at having to explain to King.

He answered her call on the second ring, his voice deep and strong, the voice of a man who could take on the world and come out fighting.

'King! It's Mitch! We're…' Quickly she acquainted him with their exact location. 'He's got his chair stuck in a rut and he seems to have come out without his medication. It's for his breathing. I think it's—'

'I know where it is,' he rasped, and that was it. He was on his way before she even had time to cut the call.

Rayne couldn't have been more grateful when she heard the throb of the Lamborghini's engine. Through the trees she saw the car practically skid to a halt and she went weak with relief when King leapt out and raced towards them without bothering to close the door.

'Thank heaven you're here!' she breathed.

It was with immense gratitude that she relinquished the handles of the chair into his stronger and more capable hands.

'Keep clear of this,' he ordered, and with his efficient and determined strength managed to bring the man and his chair back onto even ground.

How effortlessly he had saved the day, Rayne marvelled, with tears of relief biting behind her eyes now that the ordeal was over.

'You should never have brought him out here,' he admonished after he'd overseen Mitch take his medication and was now pushing him back to the car. 'Or at the very least you should have told me where you were going.'

'He didn't want me to,' Rayne argued, refusing to be the whipping boy for two very indomitable males.

'Then you should have refused to drive him. Or at least used your own initiative to let me know where you were going.'

'It wasn't her fault.' Mitch sent a scowling upward glance back over his shoulder at his son. 'And stop talking about me like I wasn't here. That isn't like you, King. Anyway, I wanted some freedom. I get sick and tired of people fussing over me. Rayne doesn't fuss over me,' he expanded surprisingly, without looking at her as she trooped along beside them, still feeling shaken, and now unjustly chastened, by King's flaying tongue.

'I really didn't know he was going to get me to drive him here,' she admitted, trying to placate him, sensing he was still angry with her after he had got his father and his chair back into the Bentley and was now moving back to his own car. 'But I couldn't go against his wishes and tell you he was going out. He's got so much pride, King. Almost as much as you,' she tagged on by way of an accusation, surprising herself by defending Mitch. 'He feels humiliated asking you to do the simplest things he used to do himself,' she uttered with angry tears welling up in her from those frightening moments when she'd been hanging on to that chair, sick with worry over Mitch Clayborne's state of health. 'Have you never felt humiliated by anything?'

She looked like a warring goddess, King thought, seeing her eyes dancing like splintering emeralds and her tousled red hair falling wildly round her shoulders as her beautiful body squared in decisive challenge against him. But those tears were genuine, and the fierceness with which she was standing up for his father touched him in a way he didn't want to be touched.

One stride was all it took and he was reaching for her.

'It's all right,' he reassured her, enfolding her in his arms and feeling her slender body shaken by sobs. 'It's all right. There's no harm done,' he murmured into her perfumed hair.

It seemed so right to cling to him, Rayne thought, steadied by his hard warmth. He seemed so dependable and strong. So much so that she wanted to stay there with her head resting against his shoulder while she breathed in his very masculine scent and felt the heavy beat of his heart drumming against hers.

But that was just a flight of fancy because of all she'd been through this morning, she told herself. Because she needed someone and he just happened to be here.

'I've got to get Mitch home,' she said huskily, pulling herself free, and tripped across to the Bentley without a glance back.

In her room the following evening, Rayne paced the tastefully patterned tiles, reflecting on the previous day's events.

That episode with Mitch had been scary, but so had those traitorous feelings she'd experienced during those few crazy moments in King's arms.

Sexual attraction was one thing. You didn't have to know or even like someone very much to feel its unmistakable and often dangerous tug. But what she had felt when King had shown that tender and more understanding side of his nature yesterday had been thoroughly more bewildering and complicated.

She was there to get an admission—and through the tabloids if Mitch refused to comply with what she wanted—and getting emotionally involved with King Clayborne wasn't on her agenda. Even if Mitchell Clayborne thought it should be!

'Is there something you're not telling me, Rayne?' he had

asked her after she'd pulled out of King's arms and climbed into the Bentley yesterday.

'No, I don't think so,' she'd refuted, knowing full well he was referring to the embrace he had just witnessed between them.

'Pity,' he'd expressed, although that unusual glint in his watery blue eyes had assured her he didn't believe her. 'You'd be a good match for him. He needs someone who'll stand up to him once in a while, and I must admit it would be no hardship to me if you were to stick around.'

Which she definitely wasn't going to! Rayne thought now, with the same stab of guilt she'd felt yesterday in realising that she was unintentionally getting herself caught up in Mitch's affections.

She was getting far too involved with both men, and she had never intended that, she thought despairingly. The longer she stayed, the more she was becoming embroiled in their everyday lives, their worries, their concerns and, where King was concerned, she didn't even have to spell out the problem to herself there.

Quite simply, that crazy fever she had been suffering from as a hapless teenager had returned in full force, threatening to consume her with its intensity because she had no protection against it. His cruel words and actions then should have immunized her for life, and she thought they had until she had met him again the other night. How he made her feel was like an ever-changing strain of some deadly virus that couldn't be controlled, and the second time around it was even more potent and deadly than the first. It didn't help either, telling herself that she was a woman now and therefore should have known better. Known how to ride the torments of this lethal attraction until it passed. Because it wouldn't, she was shocked to realise. Because the only drug that would alleviate her symptoms was in the full-blown act of his possession of her. And then the relief, she thought, would only be short-lived, because once she had allowed herself to cross that line with him she knew she would never be able to have enough of King Clayborne. Like a drug, after its effects had worn off, the symptoms would return until she could indulge herself again, which would mean taking him into her until she could feel his power and his energy filling her up and seeping into every clamouring cell of her body, by which time she would be a hopeless addict.

No, she resolved, coming to a standstill at last on the beautiful pale Indian rug and making her decision.

First thing in the morning, she determined with a sudden painful contraction of her stomach muscles, she was going to let them both know exactly who she was and what she was doing there.

CHAPTER FIVE

'MONSIEUR CLAYBORNE? *Non*, he is not up yet,' the house-keeper informed Rayne when she enquired where he was. 'And Monsieur King...' Hélène Dupont always referred to him as that, Rayne noticed, as though to call him simply 'King' would somehow detract from the respect she felt he commanded '...I believe he is still giving an interview on the terrace.'

'An interview?' Rayne queried, her curiosity aroused.

'It's to do with the documentary he is sponsoring. The one about clean water for some African villages. I believe he is heavily committed to that. They rang early. It was unexpected,' Hélène told her before concluding, 'I think he will be about half an hour more.'

'Thanks,' Rayne responded, her smile strained, her insides knotted up, as they had been almost continuously since she'd made her decision to tell the truth, so much so that she'd scarcely slept last night.

Finding out about the charitable work that King was involved in didn't make her feel any better about deceiving him. In fact, it made her feel a whole lot worse.

She hadn't, until now, even considered him having a compassionate side. Not really compassionate. Not until he had comforted her on that cliff-top the other morning. But then hadn't he seen to it that her mother got her flowers when she was having difficulty ordering them? And rushed back from New York as soon as he'd been alerted to his father's state of health?

But then again, perhaps his main reason for coming back from New York was to suss her out, Rayne reflected disparagingly. After all, he'd already been forewarned that she was there. And as for the flowers? Well, he wanted to get her into bed, didn't he? And there could be other reasons for wanting to help people less fortunate than oneself. Like the publicity, for starters.

With his influence and money he could easily afford to help fund an irrigation programme for people in Africa. And it wouldn't do his company's image any harm at all to have favourable deeds associated with the Clayborne name.

And now she was being as cynical as he was, she thought, in willing herself to believe those things about him when, had she not known him better, and particularly after what Hélène had told her, she would have said he was a man of principle— a man who wouldn't stoop to stealing another man's intellectual property and helping to ruin his life.

But he had, she thought bitterly, standing there at the foot of the stairs and closing her eyes against the truth. That Kingsley Clayborne, the man who had broken her heart as a teenager and who now had her craving his attentions with every weak, betraying cell in her body, just wasn't the man she wanted him to be.

Half an hour later, Mitch still hadn't put in an appearance and King was still tied up with his visitor on the terrace.

Coming downstairs again into the deserted opulence of the sitting room, Rayne could still hear their muted voices drifting in from the sun-soaked terrace. The male interviewer's tones were rather even and uninteresting in contrast to the deeper, richer modulations of King's.

How could any woman not find herself drawn to him and in the most fundamental way? Rayne wondered, listening to him. When everything about him was unadulterated perfection? The way he looked, the way he conducted himself, the way he dressed. That sexy yet authoritative voice that had the power to make every woman he spoke to go weak at the knees.

Then there were the other traits of his personality, too. Determination and drive and that restless energy about him that made up the whole man, and amounted to a pretty formidable package which made him impossible to ignore.

In fact it gave her goosebumps all over her body, just as it was doing now. Goosebumps and a multitude of nervous flutters in her stomach from the thought of what she had to do and the consequences of what telling him the truth might be.

Hearing the scrape of chairs on the terrace, accompanied by phrases that warned her that the interview was drawing to a close, suddenly Rayne lost her nerve. Wasn't it Mitch she should be confronting first anyway?

She had almost reached the stairs when she caught the sound of the men's footsteps across the tiled floor and she quickened her own, keen to get away before they reached the hall.

'Oh, Rayne…' Too late, the honeyed resonance of King's voice drifted towards her, lifting the hairs at the nape of her neck, exposed by her loosely piled-up hair. 'Have you seen Hélène?'

'Not for some time,' she said shakily, turning round, her breath locking from the impact of his dark-suited executive image, from his poised elegance and commanding stature.

Why was it that other men seemed to diminish beside him? she wondered with painful awareness. She had only a fleeting impression of his younger, shorter companion because her gaze was held—against her will, it seemed—by the steel-blue snare of King's.

Beneath her simple white top and jeans, her body pulsed from the pull of his powerful magnetism and it wasn't until he broke the contact to say something to his tawny-haired visitor that Rayne, remembering her manners, turned to speak to the man.

As she did so, her greeting, like her smile, died on her lips and Rayne could feel her blood starting to run cold.

'What are *you* doing here?' the interviewer asked.

'Do you two know each other?' King enquired with a rather quizzical expression.

Rayne wanted to deny it, her mind chaotically processing what the chances were of the journalist who'd come to interview King being someone from her past. And not just someone. But Nelson Faraday!

'We worked together,' she admitted when she could wrench her tongue from the roof of her mouth, hoping against hope that the slick-talking journalist wouldn't give her away, not before she'd had the chance to do it herself.

'In what capacity?' King asked, still wearing that interested smile, but behind the urbane veneer Rayne could sense every sharp instinct honing in like a stalking tiger's.

'I was the office junior,' Rayne put in quickly. 'When I started, Nelson here was already destined for greater things.' So great that she'd packed him up after only a couple of evenings out with him because she hadn't liked his cut-throat methods of reporting. But this man knew more about her than was comfortable. In fact, it was downright mortifying, Rayne thought, in view of where she was and who she was with.

'You're too modest,' her ex-colleague told her, much to Rayne's overriding dread and dismay, because it was clear the man had picked up on her reluctance to talk. She could tell he was assessing what she might be doing in this billionaire's pad and, from the way his eyes took in both her and King, knew that his mind was already working overtime. 'She might have been the office junior when she started out on that provincial little rag, but everyone could see she had the nose of a bloodhound and that once she'd got going there'd be no one to touch Lorrayne Hardwicke for sniffing out a scoop.'

It was clear Nelson Faraday was still holding a grudge, Rayne realised, horrified, her eyes darting guardedly towards King.

There was tension in his jaw and in the sudden granite-like mask of his features. His cheekbones seemed to stand out prominently beneath the olive of his skin.

'Oh, dear...' The other man was putting up a good show of looking shamefaced, because he couldn't have failed to notice the atmosphere that had grown cold enough to freeze the heat of the Mediterranean day. 'Did I say something I shouldn't have?' he remarked with an award-winning performance of mock innocence.

'No, of course not,' Rayne put in quickly, wise to Nelson Faraday's tactics and to what he must be thinking. That she was either romantically involved with Clayborne's dynamic helmsman or she was there to dig up some dirt on the family. Which was too close to the truth, she thought, with her heart frantically pumping.

'You certainly didn't,' King remarked with a pasted-on smile, the cynicism with which he said it making Rayne shiver.

'Well, it's lovely seeing you again, Lorrayne.' The younger man was backing away, his eyes suddenly wary beneath the implacable steel of King's. 'I'll forward a copy of the article to you, sir.' Nelson was lapsing into total deference, as he always had with his most prized interviewees, and King Clayborne had to be among his most prized of all.

'You do that.' King's tone was clipped, lethally low.

His anger was roused and she was about to bear the brunt of it, Rayne realised, knowing she deserved no less. Knowing she should have told him—told them both—from the start.

Like a coward, though, as soon as the other man had left, she started towards the stairs, wanting to get away from King until he had calmed down.

'Oh, no, you don't!' Strong fingers suddenly clamped onto

her wrist, preventing her precipitous flight up the stairs. 'So you're Lorri Hardwicke. Well, well.'

'Let me go!' She could feel his white hot anger pulsing against her as those determined fingers tightened relentlessly around her soft flesh. 'I was going to tell you! Both of you!' she gasped as he pulled her towards him.

'You were? Well, that's very magnanimous of you!' he scorned. 'And when exactly were you going to do that? When you'd got your "scoop", or whatever it is you're after? What exactly is it you're after, Rayne?' His face was livid, his voice so dangerously soft that with one fearful yet furious yank she managed to pull free.

'What was rightfully my father's!' she shot up at him, massaging her wrist, numb from the pressure he'd applied.

'And what is that?' he breathed equally softly, every long lean inch of him powerfully intimidating, like a dangerous adversary she'd been unfortunate to cross. Well, he wasn't going to intimidate *her!*

'You know very well!' There were family loyalties at stake here. 'You stole that software from him! You and Mitch! You knew MiracleMed was his and you stole it!'

'And you, my dear young woman, have been very much misinformed if you think you can make a serious allegation like that.'

'I haven't been misinformed! I know the hours he put in— at home, as well as in the office. And don't speak to me like that. I don't need to be patronized by you!'

'Just the pleasure I can give that beautiful body when it suits you.'

'No!' Shame washed over her like scalding water.

'Don't deny it, Rayne. You're as enslaved by your desire for me as I am for you. Or was that all part of the act?' he tossed at her roughly.

'No!' What could she say? How on earth had they got on to this? 'That…that just happened,' she stammered, stepping back as he moved nearer, knowing that even now, if he touched her, she would have no defence or resistance against his particular brand of humiliation. And it would be humiliation. He'd make certain of that.

'I'll bet it did! And I'll bet you've been laughing all the way to the bank in thinking I was so taken in.'

'You were never taken in.'

'Maybe not. But Mitch was. So what is it you want?' he demanded. 'Money?'

'That's the only thing that matters to people like you, isn't it?' She was near to tears, but tears of anger and frustration which had been bottled up for so long. 'Well, it might surprise you to know that some of us put honour and respect before making ourselves rich at other people's expense.'

'Really?' A masculine eyebrow arched in obvious derision. 'There didn't seem to be much honour and respect in the way you engineered your scheming little way into this house. Those thieves didn't take your passport, did they, Rayne?'

His question, so direct and demanding, seemed to suck the air right out of her body. King Clayborne might be a lot of things, but a fool wasn't one of them.

'No,' she answered, inhaling again. 'It was in the glove compartment of the car with my driving licence.'

'And your credit cards? Where have they been while Mitch and I have been financing your every requirement? Your meals. Trips into town. The flowers for your poor ailing mother?'

The disparaging way he referred to Cynthia Hardwicke sent anger coursing through Rayne in red-hot shafts.

'My mother has been sick! Very sick!' she retorted fiercely. 'And don't you ever dare to refer to her illness like that again! And my credit cards *were* stolen! They took my bag. My traveller's cheques. All my money. Everything! It was only when Mitch jumped to the conclusion that I'd lost my passport as well and invited me back here that…well… that I let him think so. I felt he owed it to me. Or to Dad at least.' And it was her father who had said that windows of opportunity didn't just open on their own—that you had to create them. 'I needed to talk to him but I knew it wouldn't be easy, and it just seemed like the perfect chance I'd been waiting for.'

'I'll bet it did! So what have you been hoping to gain out of all this if, as you say, you're far too honourable to contemplate blackmailing him with the threat of selling some cracked-up story to the papers? Are you in league with this Faraday character? Is that it? Was that why he turned up here so coincidentally today?'

'That *was* only coincidence,' she retorted with bright wings of colour staining her cheeks. 'And I wasn't going to blackmail Mitch. I was hoping—if I could talk to him—let him know who I was and what my father went through—that it might prick his conscience in some way. That I might be able to appeal to his better nature.' Hotly then, she couldn't help adding, 'I didn't imagine for one moment I could ever appeal to yours!'

'So why didn't you tell him who you were? Right away? The day you got here?' he interrogated, ignoring her last derogatory remark about himself. 'Or was the prospect of sharing a house with such a newsworthy name too much for your journalistic instinct to pass up?'

'I didn't because he seemed so shaken up after those lads had taken his wheel,' she answered, ignoring him in turn, even though she was railing inside at his high-and-mighty attitude, 'I didn't want to do or say anything that might have upset him even more. And the day after that he still wasn't well.' And then you arrived, she remembered with her mouth firming in rebellion, although she didn't tell him that. Didn't let on that she feared and regarded him with far more respect than she feared and regarded his father, not least because of the frightening strength of her attraction to him. 'And then when Hélène said he had a heart problem and high blood pressure...' Her shoulder lifted in a kind of hopeless gesture. 'I didn't want to be responsible for making him ill.'

A thick eyebrow was lifting again in patent scepticism. 'Do I detect a conscience, Rayne? Surely not! And you'll have to excuse me,' he tagged on, with no hint of apology in his voice. 'It's Lorri, isn't it? But then it's difficult keeping up with the change of identity.'

'It isn't a change of identity. Rayne Carpenter's the name I write under,' she said, admitting it now.

'Why? So that your victims won't know who you are when they read the sensationalist dirt you've managed to dredge up about them?'

'I don't write that sort of news story.' Chance would have been a fine thing! She had never got beyond covering house-fires started from flaming chip pans and local demonstrations about library closures, whatever Nelson Faraday had led him to believe. 'I only write the truth.'

'Or your warped version of it.'

'Is it warped to expect some credit for my father's work? I'm not after any personal or financial gain, whatever you may think.'

'No. Just making strong allegations about a man who isn't well enough to defend himself. Well, I'll defend him, Lorri. And you'll find I'm not half so weak—or so smit-ten—as my father is. Grant Hardwicke did a lot of the work on MiracleMed. I believe I'm right in saying that. But he did it under a corporate umbrella.'

'Which was what you told him the night you came round and threatened him!' she reminded him. 'And just for want-ing recognition for what was rightfully his! He created that software long before he ever joined forces with Mitch. He just didn't have the resources to launch it. He was honest and hardworking and never cheated or lied to anyone in his entire life. And you made him ill,' she uttered, aggrieved, and with such painful emotion in her voice it was difficult to breathe. 'You and Mitch! He might still have been alive today if you hadn't!'

Though she was saying it, some small part of her acknowledged that it wasn't strictly true. That there were other events that had contributed to the strain her father had been under. Like his bouts of drinking that had only made their family life harder. And the way he'd seemed to lose the will to do anything—even look for a job towards the end—which had only added to his increasing sense of worthlessness.

'I admire your loyalty to your father,' King surprised her by expressing. 'But I didn't see him as quite the paragon of virtue you obviously did. We're all human, dearest, and Grant Hardwicke could be as opportunistic and self-motivated as the next man.'

'That's a lie!'

'Is it?' King's mouth was a tight, inexorable line. Looking back, he still couldn't believe the man's crocodile tears when he'd told him about Mitch's accident. But then he hadn't been crying for Mitch—his closest friend and colleague. All he'd been concerned about was his own personal losses and all he might have stood to lose if his accusations of theft had ever been brought to the public's notice. 'Far be it from me to want to hurt you, but I can be every bit as ruthless as you're accusing me of being if—'

He broke off abruptly as a flushed-faced Hélène suddenly came rushing down the stairs towards them, her features looking pinched within their frame of greying bobbed hair. 'Oh, *monsieur*! You had better come quickly. It's Monsieur Clayborne!' Her hand went to her chest. 'He has the pain...'

King was springing away from them without any further prompting, taking the open staircase two steps at a time.

He was already at his father's bedside when Rayne raced up to Mitch's room with the housekeeper close behind her. One look at the elderly man who was sitting on the edge of the bed, still only half-dressed, revealed that he was in extreme pain.

'Call an ambulance!' King directed urgently towards Hélène.

While the housekeeper was summoning help on the bedroom telephone, Rayne hurried over to the bed.

Oh, please! she prayed. *Let him be all right! Don't let it be my fault that this has happened!*

'He needs to lie back,' she instructed, sensing that this was one occasion when King needed someone's help and advice, with all her basic first aid training rushing to the fore. And when he looked at her questioningly, 'It's all right. I know what I'm doing,' she assured him, suggesting how he could help, already plumping pillows and generally helping to make his father as comfortable as she could. Now wasn't the time to tell him how she had taken a first aid course after her father had died, when she'd read how anyone could make a difference in a medical emergency.

Glad that at least she hadn't contributed to this situation by actually telling Mitch who she really was, she watched King through eyes suddenly blurry with relief, gently easing his father back against the pillows, catching his deep, low murmurs of reassurance—despite his own concern—as he tried to put the older man's mind at rest.

Oh, to have him speak to her with that depth of emotion! She felt a surge of longing that was quite out of place in the current situation, or within the bounds of anything approaching logic. Why did she want anything more from him other than—as he'd pointed out to her downstairs—the pleasure her body craved from him? Surely she wasn't allowing herself to think of him in any capacity beyond that? Because if she were, she warned herself harshly, then she was being a total fool.

The ambulance didn't take long to arrive.

'Can I come with you?' Rayne appealed to King, hot on

his heels as he flew down the stairs while the medical team were bringing Mitch down in the lift.

'You?' he emphasised, his expression a contrary mix of surprise and blinding objection. She had been quick to help his father, King thought. And she looked concerned. Genuinely upset. But with a woman—particularly this woman—who could tell? 'That won't be necessary,' he told her succinctly, leaving her staring after his dark retreating figure and feeling as though she had been slapped in the face.

'What is it, King?' Mitchell Clayborne was staring at his son's broad back as King in turn stood staring out of the window of the private clinic. 'God knows I haven't been the best of fathers, but I would have thought the news that I'm not going to be consigned to the history books just yet would have made you a bit happier than you seem.'

Sighing heavily, King dragged himself away from an absent study of the clear evening sky, his mouth pulling down on one side at his father's dry remark. Mitch certainly sounded better, and his breathing was easier than it had been a few hours ago, but he had no intention of causing the man any undue distress.

'It's nothing that can't wait,' he answered.

'And it's nothing that I'm not man enough to take—even wired up like a puppeteer's blasted dummy! Tell me.'

It was clear to King that the man would be more likely to die of a heart attack from being kept in suspense rather than from being told the truth.

'It's about Rayne,' he breathed, the air seeming to shiver through his nostrils.

'What about her?' Mitch brought his head off the mountain of pillows, suddenly looking alarmed. 'She's all right, isn't she?'

King nodded. He couldn't believe how fond of her his father had become.

'What, then?' Mitch demanded with considerably less than his usual strength.

King hesitated, but only briefly. 'She's Lorri Hardwicke,' he stated, drawing another deep breath.

Mitch stared at him for a long worrying moment before closing his eyes.

'Shouldn't I have realised it!' he exclaimed somewhat breathlessly at length, with an unusual tremor in his gravelly voice.

'Do you know why she's here?'

'I think I can guess,' Mitch returned. 'But tell me anyway.'

'She's saying what Grant said all those years ago. That Claybornes took the credit for MiracleMed when it really belonged to him. In short, she's accusing us—but you in particular—of, at best, gross professional misconduct and, at worst, outright theft.'

Had he gone too far? King wondered anxiously, wanting to kick himself for telling him when he saw the pain that darkened Mitch's eyes and heard the way his breathing had suddenly became more laboured.

'She's right, King.'

'What?' Above the sound of footsteps hurrying along the corridor outside and the intermittent bleep of Mitch's monitoring machine, King's response was one of almost inaudible shock.

'I did steal that software.'

King's face was sculpted with harsh lines of bewilderment. 'What are you saying?' he whispered, his face turning pale, his mouth contorting in revulsion and disbelief.

'It's true,' Mitch admitted heavily. 'I know you thought I put a lot of my own time into it, but I didn't. I'm glad it's out. I'm glad you know, King. It's been hell keeping it to myself— and from you in particular—all of these years.'

For once King found himself unable to think straight. Had he really heard Mitch correctly? Was his own father admitting to being a thief? Was that what had been gnawing away at him for so long? Making him so bitter?

'You let me—let everyone—believe he produced the whole thing in the company's time. Or a large part of it, anyway. Under Clayborne's corporate umbrella!' King reminded him roughly.

'It was his word against mine—and he had no proof.'

'So you took it on yourself to call it yours? Another man's intellectual property!' King stared at his father, appalled. 'Didn't it occur to you that you might be robbing him of his livelihood? That he had dependants? A wife and a daughter?'

'So she's come after me,' Mitch murmured, sounding far away, as though he wasn't listening. 'After all these years! What a sparky little thing.'

'She's deceitful!' King rasped, feeling his earlier anger brewing, although he wasn't sure any more whether to be angry with her as well as his father, or just with himself. 'What I hadn't realised until now was that you were. My own father!'

He swung away towards the window again, massaging his neck, sightlessly watching the glittering sky mellowing with the lateness of the day. He didn't want to be speaking to his father like that. Not while he was so unwell.

He hadn't wanted to speak to Rayne as he had either, but the shock of discovering who she was with the knowledge that he had not only been ensnared by her beautiful face and body, but had also been made a fool of into the bargain had been much too much for his masculine self-esteem to take all in one go.

He couldn't forget though how fiercely she had defended Grant Hardwicke, standing up for him with all the loyalty and determination of a loving daughter. Nor could he forget the emotion in her face when she had asked him if she could come here today and he had point-blank refused to let her. After she had helped his father, too. After she could so easily have turned away and not got involved. Although she hadn't, he reflected, even though only minutes before she had been accusing Mitch of committing the worst possible corporate crime against her father. And in that, he thought, with his big body stiffening, she had been right...

'King?'

The weak appeal had him reluctantly turning to regard the semi-reclining form on the bed, the tension so gripping in his shoulders that he thought his spine would snap.

'Why?' he demanded of his father, his strong features ravaged by a complexity of emotions. 'Why did you do it, damn you? Why, Mitch?'

Amazingly, there was contrition and sadness too, King noted, in the watery blue eyes looking out of his father's loose-skinned, rather florid face. 'Do you—of all people—really need to ask?' He looked away, towards the ceiling and the metal curtain track that ran around his bed, sighing heavily. 'You *know* why.'

CHAPTER SIX

THE sky was changing from molten gold to burnished crimson.

In the grounds surrounding the house and on the forested hillside the crickets had struck up their shrill evening chorus, while in the distance, way below, Monte Carlo was waking up for the night.

From the terrace, her hand on the sun-warmed stone of the balustrade, Rayne watched the lights gradually come on in the hotels and apartments, and in the cafés and bars along the coast.

A thousand stars shining almost as brightly as the planet whose light seemed to be winking at her above the dark pointed spear of a cypress tree. One lonely star in a flaming universe, Rayne thought, which was how she felt right at that moment since Hélène had taken herself off to her rooms at least an hour ago, and Rayne hadn't heard anything from King since he'd left with his father and the paramedics that morning.

A sharp breath escaped her as she heard the low growl of a car turning in through the gates, which she couldn't see from the house as it was hidden by trees, and the next second saw the Lamborghini coming along the drive. The car drew up and her heart leapt when she saw King get out and hand his keys to a member of staff to garage it for the night.

She heard their muffled voices, King's low and congenial, the other man's infused with courtesy and yet genuine respect for his mega-rich, mega-influential employer. King was his employer, she had no doubt about that, since Hélène had told her that he oversaw most of his father's affairs these days.

She had tried ringing his cellphone several times to find out how Mitch was, but if it wasn't engaged it had been on voicemail. The one message she had left around lunchtime, asking King to call her, hadn't been answered, and Hélène hadn't been able to tell her anything beyond the fact that Mitch was still having tests.

Watching King's dark head disappear under the portico, she waited, breath held, for him to come into the house. A few moments later she swung round with her heart leaping absurdly as she caught the sound of his light footsteps moving towards her over the terrace.

'How's Mitch?' she asked without any preamble.

Bracing herself for some sarcastic response about her caring, his appearance, nevertheless, made her whole body go weak.

He was still dressed in the white shirt and dark suit trousers he had been wearing that morning, but his jacket was hooked over one shoulder. He was tie-less now and his shirt with the two top buttons unfastened was unusually crumpled. His hair looked as if he had been raking it back all day, but now there were dark strands falling loosely across his forehead as if he had finally given up trying to control it. His strong jaw was darkened by a day's growth of stubble and there were dark hairs curling over the open V of his shirt.

Never had she seen him look so dishevelled, Rayne realised. Nor so utterly and sensationally male.

'He had an angina attack. It wasn't a coronary.' The relief with which he informed her of that was almost tangible.

'So he's going to be all right?'

His eyes tugged over the golden slope of her shoulders beneath the shoelace straps of her dress, and Rayne felt as if the fine white chiffon would melt beneath the searing steel of his eyes.

'Do you truly care?' he murmured, so softly that she might have misheard him as he tossed his jacket unceremoniously down onto one of the heavily cushioned dining seats.

'Of course I care. I left a message,' she told him a little sharply, 'but you didn't answer.'

Because he hadn't known what to say to her after their antagonised scene this morning. Hadn't known then—when he was at the hospital—or now—when he was faced with the reality of telling her—exactly how to deal with the things his father had told him.

He merely dipped his head in acknowledgement of what she had said.

'They're keeping him in for observation, but hopefully he's going to be all right.'

He looked so weary—devastated, almost, Rayne would have said—that she had the strongest urge to go over and put her arms around him in the way he'd done with her the other day. Tell him that she understood the anguish in having a sick parent—of losing a parent, even—but she held back. This was King Clayborne, after all. Hard. Impervious. Impenetrable. And he had found her out in the web of deceit she'd been weaving ever since she'd been here. He'd have no sympathy for her. Or any member of her family.

Steeling herself against that imperviousness with her head held stiffly, she enquired, 'Have you come back to ask me to leave?'

'No.'

No? Surprise pleated her forehead. 'I thought you wouldn't be able to get rid of me fast enough.'

'That's what I thought,' he admitted with a heavy sigh.

Rayne's frown deepened. 'What's changed your mind? Or do you just want to keep me here to extract some sort of payment from me for lying to you?'

He came over to lean on the balustrade, looking out towards the sea beyond the twilit city. He chuckled softly, an almost self-derisory sound. 'What sort of man do you imagine I am, Lorrayne?'

She couldn't answer at first because all the replies that sprang to mind weren't very complimentary. And because he was so near that she could feel the power of his masculinity emanating from him, smell the faint hint of his animal scent beneath the lingering traces of his cologne.

'Tough. Determined. Implacable.' Her mouth pulled slightly as she finished reeling them off.

He made another self-deprecating sound down his nostrils as he angled his body towards her, his forearm resting on the still warm stone. 'Why do I get the impression that those adjectives were carefully chosen from the best of a bad bunch?'

Because they were, she thought, but remained silent this time.

'You also thought I was grossly unscrupulous in being party to some treacherous and probably very unlawful act against your father,' he stated, straightening up, 'but I want you to know categorically now that I wasn't.'

Strangely, she believed him, Rayne realised, shocked. But there was no room for anything other than truth in the deep intensity of his voice, nor, she accepted with a pulse-quickening heat stealing through her as she brought her head up, in the disturbing clarity of his eyes.

'And Mitch?' She looked quickly seaward to avoid his penetrating gaze, fixing hers on the light-spangled silhouette of a cruise ship moored way out in the distant harbour. 'Did you tell him who I was?'

Her voice was infused with resentment, King noted. Something she had held against Mitch—against *him*—for years. 'He knows who you are,' he disclosed.

'And what did he say?' She looked up at him again now, her lovely face pained and accusing. 'Did he admit that

MiracleMed was Dad's? And that he snatched it from under his nose?'

King took a deep breath. 'It wasn't quite like that, Lorri.'

'No?' Her head was tilted in rebellious challenge and her hair was as fiery as the Monte Carlo sunset. 'How was it?' she bitterly invited him to tell her.

King glanced away, way down across the scintillating Principality, watching a stream of red tail lights form a blur of colour along the highway following the curve of the coast.

This day had wreaked havoc on him, if any day could. First finding out that Rayne was Lorri Hardwicke. Then Mitch's suspected heart attack. And, to add to all that, those soul-sinking moments at the clinic when he'd believed his father was the worst kind of criminal. But Mitch's sin had been a moral one, rather than anything illegal. Even so, it still offended King's sense of propriety to realise that Grant Hardwicke had been treated so unfairly. And it wasn't going to be easy telling his daughter the truth when, either way, she wasn't going to want to hear the answer.

'Your father signed an agreement with Mitch just after they went into partnership together, to the effect that any work done for the company while they were directors of the company would be to the benefit of the company. I know. I've read the clause in that agreement. I had my secretary email it through to me today. Your father was the technical whiz-kid, but was lax when it came to business dealings or keeping vital records. If he hadn't been, he would have registered his right in that software prior to signing that agreement, but he didn't, which was a pity,' he said, sounding as though he meant it. 'And much to his cost, as it turned out.'

'And that's it?' she queried in protest. 'He signed his rights away and it's a pity! Why? Because it made Claybornes so much money!'

'Lorrayne, stop,' King advised gently, understanding her pain, her justified anger and bitterness. He wished he hadn't learned from Mitch today that he could have acknowledged the other man's concept of that software and that he had chosen not to. It had been an act of vengeance against a man who had been his friend and whom he had wound up hating. 'No one could have quite foreseen the impact that MiracleMed would make after it was launched.'

'But it did!' she complained. 'And Dad never received any credit for it!'

'And, believe me, no one regrets that more than I do,' King said somberly.

He didn't add that, for what it was worth, Mitch now regretted it too. That would be like openly admitting his father's wrongdoing, and if Mitch wanted to apologise to her then it was up to Mitch to do it himself.

He didn't know why his father had suddenly burdened him with this today, unless it was because he'd feared he was going to die and wanted to get it off his chest. But at least he could understand now why his father had become so bitter, and how shouldering such a weight of remorse could have contributed to making him ill.

'OK. So there's nothing I can do about it now,' she accepted grudgingly, 'because it was all signed, sealed and delivered legally! But that doesn't alter the fact that your father came by that software immorally and very conveniently, after that quarrel he obviously instigated, which made Dad walk out. And I know it wasn't Dad's fault, because Dad never quarrelled with anyone!'

'For heaven's sake, Lorri, stop being so naïve!'

'Naïve?' She gave a brittle little laugh. 'You think I don't know my own father?'

'Apparently not.'

She sent a sidelong glance up at him. 'What's that supposed to mean?' she bit out with her eyes narrowing.

'It means that, much as I believe my father exercised his rights under that agreement—whether ethically or other-

wise—I also believe that it's time you, my misinformed little kitten, heard a few home truths about what really broke
up their partnership.'

'I already know that,' Rayne tossed back assuredly. 'It
was professional jealousy. He knew what Dad had created
was going to be worth a fortune and he wanted to reap all the
rewards for it himself!' She couldn't believe she was saying
things like this about Mitch Clayborne. The man who had
taken her in. Offered her food and shelter and a safe haven
to get her affairs sorted out when she'd found herself virtually stranded so far from home.

'Jealousy, maybe. But not so much professional as deeply
personal, I imagine,' King was saying with a grim cast to his
features. 'My father quarrelled with yours because of the affair Grant was having with Mitch's wife.'

'You're lying!' She couldn't believe King could dream up
something so despicable.

'Am I? Then why do you think there were never any proper
claims made by your father to try and secure the rights to
his software?'

'Because you threatened him! I was there when you did
it!' she reminded him passionately.

'And you think that was enough to stop him pursuing any
claim against the company if he thought he could have, unless he hadn't something to hide?'

She wanted to protest, but his words rang with something
so akin to the truth that they left her speechless. There were
times when she had wondered why her father hadn't fought
harder to try and get the rights to MiracleMed into his name.
Sometimes she had begged him to, but he hadn't, and she'd
thought it was because he just hadn't had any fight left in him.

'I came round that night—rightly or wrongly—to tell him
to stay away from my father. I had very little else on my mind
except that my stepmother had been killed and that Mitch was
more than likely to be in a wheelchair for life. He'd known

about the affair for weeks, which had led to Grant leaving the company. But it was the shock of being told by Karen that she was leaving Mitch to run away with your father that caused him to lose control of the car that night and swerve into that tree. He was going to leave you, Lorrayne. You and your mother. The dear, devoted husband and father.' The censure which dripped through his words was evidence of just how little respect he had for Grant Hardwicke—or the institution of marriage. 'Did you really not know?'

Mortified, Rayne could only stare up at him. Finally she made a small negative gesture with her head.

How could it be true? Her parents had loved each other, she reflected achingly. Or had King been right in calling her naïve? Had Cynthia Hardwicke known? Been aware of her husband's infidelity? But no, she couldn't have been!

Painfully, she recalled her mother's constant assurance that it was Grant's memory that had given her the strength to fight through her recent illness. So what would it do to her now if she found out that all that love and devotion she'd thought he'd shown her had been just a sham? It would destroy her!

'I'm sorry I've had to be the one to destroy all your illusions about love and commitment, my dearest.'

'I'm not your dearest.' She wasn't ready yet to accept endearments from him after he had opened her eyes so cruelly.

'Maybe not,' he conceded which, contrarily, hurt her even more, 'but you're feeling bruised and cut up about it, naturally.'

How do you know how I feel? she wanted to fling at him, but bit the words back. It wasn't his fault that everything she'd believed in seemed to have crumbled to dust within the space of a few short minutes, even if it felt like it right at this moment.

She turned away from him, her hands resting limply on the top of the balustrade.

'He lied,' was all she could say, staring out at the darkening sea, hurting so much she didn't think she'd live to trust anyone ever again. 'To me. To Mum...'

'I'm sorry,' he murmured deeply. And, after a few seconds, 'Passion makes us do the most unprincipled things,' he said.

Didn't she know it!

'It's the second strongest animal force in the universe.'

'Only the second?' she uttered disdainfully.

'Perpetuation of the species.' His tone was flat—unsentimental. 'Preceded only by self-survival.'

He made it all seem so cold. So basic.

He laughed rather harshly when she told him so. 'Isn't it?' he suggested with unyielding scepticism.

'Is that all you think love is for?' she challenged, wondering how she had got on to this subject with him as she faced him again. 'Just to create babies?'

'Yes, but then we aren't actually talking about love, are we...Lorri?'

He caught her hand, his fingers strong and warm, but angrily she tugged out of their grasp.

'Don't call me that!' It was her father—her father, whom she had loved and trusted and looked up to, who had first started using that name. Everyone else had simply called her Lorrayne. 'It's Rayne to you!'

Which suited him fine, King thought, having been used to calling her that. It suited the woman she had become and who had changed so dramatically from the thin and stammering—at least with him, he remembered wryly—little scarecrow whom he'd known as Lorri, and who had graced the office for a time with her quiet presence.

'Then don't hate me, Rayne, for simply acquainting you with the facts.'

'I don't hate you.' Hate was just the flip side of a coin that suggested far too intense an emotion than she was prepared even to think about. 'Why should I hate you?'

'For knocking your gallant knight down off his horse?'

'I'm getting used to it,' she murmured with unshed tears in her eyes. Her emotions were too raw at that moment to stop herself from tagging on, 'After all, you did it to me once before.'

A frown knitted his brows as his gaze probed the moist hazel-green of hers.

'I was mad about you,' she admitted, not caring what she said any more.

'I know.'

His deep revelation shocked and surprised her. Had she been that obvious?

'You noticed me?' she breathed, having never beyond her wildest teenage dreams ever dared to hope.

'You were a child,' he remarked succinctly.

'I was eighteen!'

'As I said—a child,' he repeated with a soft chuckle, lifting her chin with his forefinger, his thumb lightly brushing her pouting lips. 'A little girl with big hungry eyes...' Because he knew now why those eyes had kept tugging at something inside him ever since that night he'd walked in and saw her standing here on the terrace. 'Huge hungry eyes,' he continued, 'that I remember thinking even then that one day some man would drown in. But which right then belonged to a love-sick teenager whose main reason for agreeing to help out in that office, I suspect, was to try and make me want to take her to bed.'

'I wasn't love-sick,' she denied with embarrassed colour flaring in her cheeks, overwrought from the feelings that had been building in her for hours because of his keeping her in suspense, because of his opinion of her father. Because she had been aching to see him—and talk to him—all day when she should have been hating him, convinced as she had been of just how ruthless he was. And when all she wanted him to do right now—and from the first moment she'd seen him walk in here tonight—really was to take her to bed. 'Anyway, if I had been, it wouldn't have worked with you, would it,' she murmured with her blood suddenly pounding in her ears because the touch of his hands sliding lightly across her shoulders and down over her bare arms seemed to be setting her insides on fire. 'Most of the time you ignored me.'

'I wasn't knocked out by spiky bleached hair and dark purple lips and eyes,' he stated with his mouth moving wryly. 'And what would you have preferred me to have done? Taken you over my knee for even thinking about it with a man way out of your age group?'

'You were only twenty-three!' she reminded him, breathless from her galloping emotions, wanting to run away from them—from him—and all the things he was saying that was sending a reckless excitement leaping through her. 'That's only five years.'

'And those five years made a world of difference,' he said sagely.

Which they would have, she accepted in hindsight.

Riveted by a desire that was stronger than her will, she looked up at him now to ask in a voice that was huskily provocative, 'So what are you saying? That I'm too young for you?'

She heard the sharp catch of his breath above the chorus of crickets and, from the lights that had just come on around the terrace, saw the sensuous pull of his lips before he answered thickly, 'Not any more.'

Common sense should have told her to stop this insanity before it got too far out of hand but, as his mouth came down over hers, it was already too late.

CHAPTER SEVEN

As KING wrapped his arms around her, Rayne felt herself melting against him.

His jaw rasped against hers where he hadn't shaved since that morning, but she rejoiced in its roughness and in his hard warmth that was driving every last trauma—of the day, of the past week and of the longer past—from her mind.

The only thing that mattered was him—here and now, the desire that had her clinging to him, as the only sure, secure thing in her crumbling universe.

She had wanted this—so much! Wanted it now a thousand times more than she had ever wanted it before. It was as if all the feelings she had had for him as a teenager hadn't died but had been shut away inside her, brooding and intensifying so that now they overwhelmed her like a flood, gushing through her from her toes upwards and spreading along every nerve and sinew of her being.

He had called her a child then, but she was a woman now and she wanted to prove it to him, angling her body so that her needs were obvious—the craving for his hands against her naked flesh.

He read her like a book, following each silent sentence her body was conveying to him as long tanned fingers slipped the fine straps off her shoulders so that the chiffon bodice rippled like a waterfall down over the betraying fullness of her breasts.

King groaned deeply in his throat, his body hardening from her perfect femininity. He felt like ravaging her, driving them both wild in his need to blot out all the things that Mitch had revealed to him today. To lose himself inside the warm, slick wetness of her glorious body. But he forced himself to exercise all his powers of restraint, knowing that she wouldn't thank him for that.

This woman needed to be handled with kid gloves, her beautiful body served and pleasured with the skill and tenderness it deserved.

She had deceived him, it was true. But only because she'd believed him to be party to a gross misdemeanour against her father—a father who hadn't been wholly worthy of her trust and fierce loyalty. Nevertheless, the fact that she *had* deceived him made him glean a delicious thrill in inflicting some sensual punishment upon her in making her wait for all her body—and his own!—craved.

Dipping his head, he drew the hard peak of one pink begging nipple slowly into his mouth, taming the urge to pull her against him as his strong hands rested on the firm, gentle curves of her straining hips.

He was driving her crazy, Rayne thought headily, clutching at his shoulders, wanting to rip off his shirt, feel the hardness of his muscles and his hair-roughened chest against her breasts.

'Easy,' he advised softly, his breath fanning the wet swollen tip he had just released from its torturous pleasure. 'What is it you want? Show me what you want.'

Maybe she should have been embarrassed, she thought distractedly, but hunger had stripped her of all inhibitions, so that now she had no qualms about doing as he'd asked.

Thrusting her neglected breast towards him, she uttered a deep, guttural sob when his mouth closed over it, sending sensations plummeting down through the centre of her body.

'Is this it?' he broke off to murmur against the pale fleshy mound after a few moments. 'Is this what you want?'

No, I want you! All of you! Around me! On top of me! Inside me!

She heard her brain screaming out those phrases and couldn't believe that any man could reduce her to thinking them. But this wasn't any man, she assured herself hectically. This was King.

His hands on her hips were warm and firm, yet still holding her away from him when all she wanted was to *feel* him, feel the evidence of just how much he wanted her.

But he was controlling the pace, she realized, wanting more of what he was doing to her and yet crazy for this particular sensuous torture to end as he burned a slick, hot path between the valley of her breasts with a teasingly slow caress of his tongue.

'I hate you, King Clayborne,' she groaned.

She could say it now. Now, when the conflagration of need that was burning inside her raged so fiercely that there could be no turning back because what was there to lose? He knew how much she wanted him. Needed him.

'No, you don't,' he murmured thickly against her ribcage.

He knew that too, she accepted helplessly, because she couldn't fool him any more than she could fool herself. But to express what she was feeling in any other way would be no less than sheer folly, she realised, despairing at herself for wanting—needing—him so much.

With a deep groan from the depths of his throat he caught her to him then, and from that moment he was no longer in control.

Hungrily his mouth captured hers, their breath mingling, tongues blending in an urgent mimicry of the ultimate outcome of where all this was leading, as Rayne let her head fall back in wanton acquiescence to all that was about to happen.

They were equal now. Mouth to mouth. Pulsing body to

pulsing body. Locked in the most fundamental act between a man and a woman.

Below them, beneath the darkening Mediterranean sky, Monte Carlo pulsed with a life of its own but they were oblivious to it, the sound of their impassioned breathing like an extension of the exotic chorus outside.

His teasing had backfired on him, Rayne realised with her heart singing. He was desperate to make love with her, a scenario she had only ever dared to dream about seven years ago. But now it was happening and the reality was sending shock waves of pleasure through her body way beyond any she could ever have imagined.

With a small sob of need and urgent trembling fingers, she tugged at the buttons of his shirt.

His chest was bronzed and beautifully contoured, as she had imagined it would be, the feathering of hair that ran down and disappeared inside his shirt igniting a fire in her as she ran her hands across it.

'You're beautiful.' It seemed as natural to say it as it did to breathe, as very softly she pressed her kiss-swollen lips to his heaving chest. He smelled of pine and a masculine musk that acted like an aphrodisiac on her already heightened senses. His skin tasted slightly salty when she brought her tongue across the hard wall of muscle and bone.

'Not nearly as beautiful as you.'

Did he really think that? Or was it just sex talking? How could she compare with the super-model type of woman his name was usually linked with? At that moment, though, she didn't care—only that he was with *her*. Like this.

'Take this off,' he urged raggedly, already tugging her dress down over her hips. 'I want to see you. All of you.'

Before she could murmur an objection, having thought about his type of woman and feeling extremely self-conscious about not living up to all he expected her to be, the whisper of fabric was nothing more than a pool of light around her ankles and she was standing there in nothing but her flimsy white sandals and a white lacy string that left very little hidden from the dark intensity of his gaze.

'King,' she breathed, hiding her sudden embarrassment against the warm hard wall of his shoulder. Gently, though, those warm strong hands held her away from him.

'Let me look at you,' he exhaled in a way that was half an entreaty, half a command.

Allowing it, she stood stock-still and closed her eyes against the starkly visual images of what she knew he would be seeing. Red hair cascading like a dark waterfall over one shoulder, the urgent rising of pale breasts with their rosy tips still hard and turgid from his exquisite attentions.

She wondered if he'd think as she did. That her breasts were slightly too full for her tiny waist and the less curvy flare of her hips. But he was smiling when she opened her eyes, the smile of a man well gratified with the gift he was being given.

He reached out then, cupping the undersides of her breasts as tenderly as if each were a rare treasure, and Rayne gave a small moan, her lashes coming down over her eyes against the excruciating pleasure that ripped through her lower body as his thumbs lightly stroked the sensitised peaks.

'Look at me.'

She didn't want to! How could she stand here like this and let him see the naked longing in her eyes? Face him, knowing that her body was betraying the extent of her need of him? But his voice was as much her master as the sensations that were holding her in thrall and very slowly her lashes fluttered apart.

He looked flushed and tousled and as much a slave to his desire as she was, she realised, feeling the burn of his gaze like a brand on her body as it slid leisurely down over her rapidly rising breasts and ribcage, over the flat plane of her belly to the white triangle of lace at the apex of her creamy thighs.

'Such loveliness should be rejoiced in. Worshipped,' he

emphasised heavily, his massaging hands leaving her breasts to follow the same path down over her midriff, her hips and her trembling thighs before coming to rest on the taut mounds of her bare buttocks, the beauty he had just spoken of with the heat of his desire bringing him finally to his knees.

Rayne gazed down on his thick dark hair as his hot mouth sought the heart of her femininity, concealed behind the last barrier of her string.

His moist heat burned into her, mingling with her hot wetness through the wisp of lace, and Rayne plunged her fingers into his hair to clutch him to her and with a groaning need thrust her throbbing centre hard against him.

He groaned his satisfaction as she squirmed above him.

'I think we can dispense with this, don't you?' he murmured huskily.

His smile was excitingly sensual when he tilted his head to look up at her, although the strong masculine face was flushed with the desire that was making his eyelids heavy and lent his mouth the brooding look of a man in the grip of passion.

Rayne sucked in her breath as his fingers made short shrift of removing the little scrap of nonsense. His hands were dark and long and extremely masculine against the smooth, silky sheen of her legs.

Blindly she saw him toss her string down alongside her dress.

Both scraps of nonsense, she thought, if she'd imagined that either could protect her from her own weakness for him, or from his potent masculinity and his determined, exciting hands.

His clothes were unbelievably arousing on her nakedness as he pulled her to him and, where she had tugged his unbuttoned shirt out of his waistband, his chest hair rasped deliciously against her swollen breasts.

'Oh, King…' Involuntarily, she was wriggling against him,

wanting even closer contact. She had never felt more wanton or more feminine.

'Easy, darling,' he said softly, and though she knew that the endearment might have been used with any woman he had been making love to, she was too driven by her need for him to be anything but happy to pretend that just for tonight she really meant something to him. 'Don't you think I feel it too?'

In fact he had never felt so hot or so hard in his entire life, King realised, with such an intense burning throb in his groin it was almost akin to pain.

He hadn't intended this when he had come back from the clinic tonight, bearing the brunt of two men's total disregard for each other. Or having to tell Rayne—while personally appalled at Mitch's lack of ethics—that, legally, she had no claim against his father, and then to go on and shatter all her illusions about love and loyalty into the bargain. But it had been a hell of a day and he needed to lose himself in the pleasure of everything she was offering. And heaven help him if he was behaving like a sex-starved teenager! But this lovely woman couldn't begin to know just how much pleasure it was going to give him to make love to her.

Claiming her mouth once more, he ground his hips against hers to show her just what she was doing to him and laughed softly into her mouth—a satisfied sound—when she gasped from the evidence of his arousal and pressed herself against his hardness in answering need.

Dragging his mouth from the drugging warmth of hers, it was only to rasp against the perfumed silk of her hair, 'Come to bed with me.'

Her murmur of acquiescence was muffled by the depth of her wanting, but he understood.

Cupping her buttocks to lift her, he felt her warm eager legs wrap around him and, like that, somehow they made it up to his suite of rooms.

Monte Carlo was a blur of lights through the panorama

of the open windows, its busy Corniche a blazing snake that led sinuously who-knew-where? Just like where making love with this man would be taking her tonight, Rayne thought distractedly, although she was in far too deep now to care.

From over his shoulder, on The Rock on the south side of the harbour, she glimpsed the palace, floodlit as a beacon against the dark velvet of the night.

Clarity against confusion. The thought rang through her brain. Like common sense against a wild, abandoned pleasure such as she had never known.

As King laid her down on the bed, she let the pleasure take her over—the excitement of him removing his clothes, the hard shadowed potency of his thrusting manhood and the heart-leaping anticipation as he came down to join her.

She reached for him at once and knew the heady thrill of touching him intimately for the first time.

'Go easy,' he advised raggedly and she could tell from his laboured breathing how close he was to losing control. 'I don't want to waste this. I want to savour every minute of these hours with you.'

That it sounded like the prelude to something final, she didn't even want to think about. She couldn't think anyway because, in moving away from her to remove her sandals, he was suddenly employing his tongue to trace a slow sensuous trail along each thigh.

Except that now he had found the secret parting between them and, lying there, breath held in shuddering anticipation, she almost screamed with pleasure when his teasing tongue flicked across her ripe swollen bud.

She had had just two lovers in her life, but she had never permitted such intimacy, and now she knew why no other relationship had ever been enough for her. Because there was only one man she wanted! Only one man she had ever wanted. And she knew that after tonight she would be spoiled for any other man who ever came after King.

As he drove her mindless with his mouth, her hands clutched the soft fabric of the coverlet beneath her to try and stem the tide of pleasure that was building in her. A small guttural murmur escaped her. She didn't want to climax yet.

'What is it? What is it you want, Rayne?' he murmured with his lips softly brushing the soft flesh of her inner thigh. They left a slick trail of warmth where they'd touched, moist from the nectar of her body.

You! her mind clamoured, begging, silently appealing to him. *It's all I've ever wanted—for so long!*

Too unsure of him to actually say as much, she used the language of her body to show him by reaching down to entice him back across her.

'Ah, is that all,' he said softly and, even in the grip of passion, she realised, there was still room for sensual teasing in his voice.

As he reached across to open the drawer of the bedside cabinet, it hit her that he was continuing to call her Rayne. Rayne, not Lorri, because Lorri, the girl he had once ignored—silly, trusting, naïve Lorri—was gone, killed off by the crumbling of everything she had trusted and believed in. By the harsh reality of life as it really was.

King's muttered oath as he pushed closed the drawer he had been groping in suddenly woke Rayne to what was wrong.

'Don't you have any?' she asked breathlessly and a little coyly, despite how far their intimacy had come.

'I thought I did.' He let out a frustrated sigh and then, with a wry pull of his mouth, 'It's been a while,' he admitted to her.

Later, Rayne would glean some comfort from that statement. Right now, though, all she felt was frustration, agonizing and raw.

'I'm sorry, Rayne.' She was lying there with her hair spread like dark fire across his pillow, her beautiful body flushed from the fever-pitch he had brought her to, and which was mirrored by the febrile glitter in her slumberous eyes. 'I should have checked.' He swore again, quite viciously this time. 'Don't look at me like that,' he said, noticing the anguish on her lovely face. 'Or you'll make me lose my mind and all my principles will be shot to the winds, and I've no intention of putting you at risk like that.'

He meant from an unwanted pregnancy.

She could see the effort it was taking for him to honour those principles he'd spoken of. His face, as he drew away from her and sat up, was ravaged by his own frustration. Even in the dim light she could see the flush that darkened the skin across his cheekbones, and his darkened jaw appeared clenched against his thwarted sexual desire. But there was a bleakness to his superb profile that made him look vulnerable and weary.

Of course, she thought, reasoning through the depths of her wanting. He had been worrying about Mitch all day...

With her heart going out to him, she wondered how she could ever have doubted that he was anything other than trustworthy, and that that integrity he was showing her now would extend to every aspect of his life. And her intuition must have recognised that for her to have still found herself so attracted to him, even when she'd wanted to believe the worst about him.

She wanted to tell him she was sorry she'd misjudged him so completely, but she was still too aroused and racked with need for him to speak. She laid tentative fingers on his forearm. 'It's all right,' she assured softly, with wild impulses leaping through her from the sensation of his skin beneath her fingers. 'We don't need one.'

'You're protected?' The disbelief that chased away some of the shadows from his face was worth a month of birthdays, Rayne thought, smiling shyly, too aroused to tell him why. That weeks ago she'd been given the Pill to correct her erratic cycle, thrown out of kilter through worrying about her mum.

'We'll be perfectly safe—I promise,' she breathed, her

simmering desire beginning to bubble over again just from caressing the superbly contoured muscle of his upper arm. It felt firm and solid. As solid as the rest of his body as he came down to her again, causing her to gasp from the weight and power of him, and then from a breath-catching expectancy as he gently parted her legs.

But he didn't enter her right away. Instead, with his hot, hard flesh merely nudging at her moist softness, he treated her to a torturous game of re-arousal that had her sobbing at the ecstasy of his tormenting lips and hands until she spread her legs fan-like and raised her hips uninhibitedly to his in a frenzied and unequivocal invitation to him to take her.

And that was more than he could take, she realised, gasping and overcome by sensation when one long, hard thrust had him sinking deeply into her eager warmth.

Pushed over the limit, she started to climax at once, bucking and sobbing until she was nothing but an abandoned mass of writhing sensations, propelled to greater and greater heights by King's driving and increasingly deeper penetration.

Her zenith when it came was a starburst of colour and spell-binding pleasure in which she felt she was being catapulted to another planet. And then the moment came when King's own climax burst and he was flowing into her, joining her with him and to him, sending the earth spinning off its axis as they floated together—one mind and one body—in some glorious parallel universe.

When she awoke, she was alone in the big bed and the blinds were drawn up to reveal the cloudless Mediterranean blue sky.

She was in a very masculine room, with plain soft furnishings and heavy designer furniture, in contrast to the pale and more delicate fitments of her own room.

Her stomach flipped now as she remembered what had

transpired, the tender spots on the most intimate places of her body an exciting reminder of a long and rapturous night.

Now, though, remembering why she had come here and all that had transpired yesterday, she wondered just how wise she had been in letting it happen.

The Claybornes had as good as destroyed her family—or at least Mitch Clayborne had, even if Grant Hardwicke *had* brought it on himself in incurring Mitch's wrath by planning to run off with his wife. But Rayne's mother wasn't aware of that, and Rayne vowed she would do her best to keep her from ever finding out. However, where King was concerned, her mother still believed, as Rayne had, that he was just as guilty as Mitch of stealing her father's work. So whatever would her mother say if she knew how little it had taken for her daughter to wind up in bed with King? She'd be horrified and hurt beyond belief, Rayne thought, as she would if she knew about Grant's affair. And how could she explain to her mother that King had played no part in hurting her father, when she didn't think Cynthia Hardwicke would even survive knowing the whole truth?

All she could do, she reasoned, was not tell her mother anything—not even let her know that she had been here.

As for Mitch Clayborne...

Turning over in bed, she let out a low groan. She didn't think she could stand the embarrassment of ever facing him again.

She was just about to step out of bed but, hearing the door opening and realising she was entirely naked, she slipped back in, pulling the single sheet up over her breasts.

Despite her concerns, her heart leaped to see King striding in wearing a white dressing gown and leather slippers. He had combed his hair, but his unshaven jaw was even darker this morning and his tanned chest and legs contrasted deeply with the robe.

'You slept well,' he commented, and his smile was so warm

that all her worries were in danger of melting like the winter's last snows. 'Hélène's cooking breakfast, but I thought you might like a glass of orange juice to revive you,' he said.

Thanking him, Rayne took the crystal glass and drank from it gratefully. She couldn't believe how thirsty she was—or how hungry. Obviously making love with him had stirred her appetites, she realised, in more ways than one.

'King… About last night,' she began when she came up for air, hardly able to look at him after all they had shared.

'What are you going to tell me?' He looked at her knowingly. 'That it shouldn't have happened?'

'Something like that,' she murmured sheepishly, finishing her juice.

'Too late, my sweet. It did.' He sounded fatalistic as he removed the empty glass from her hand. 'Not once—but twice—' his mouth was pulling sensually '—if I remember correctly. So what excuse are you going to give me for virtually ripping off my shirt and then nearly driving me out of my mind with your wicked ways?'

The dark intensity of his eyes was making her throb in every intimate part of her that he had made his own, which meant that her 'wicked ways', as he'd called them, still weren't satisfied. Because she still craved him, and even more so as she remembered every tender caress of his skilled and wonderful hands and the burning heat of his mouth on the most secret places of her body.

In a voice tremulous with desire she said, 'I didn't rip off your shirt.' And because this whole scenario was too embarrassing for her she said, 'I think I should go.'

'Go?' He frowned. 'Go where? To the bathroom? Or home?' he enquired flippantly.

'Home, of course,' she responded seriously. 'It's much too embarrassing to stay here now that Mitch knows who I am.'

'Is that the only reason?' he purred with sensuality curling his fantastic mouth again and, before she could answer, too ashamed to know how to respond, he said, 'He's expressly requested that you stay. So do I. In fact, I insist upon it.'

'Insist?' Rayne echoed with her rebellious nature surfacing through her unquenchable desire.

'All right, then. I invite you to stay,' he amended.

'Why?'

'Because I think you must be feeling a little overwrought and probably much too tired after…last night,' he reminded her with his irises darkening, although he was still smiling, 'to be in any fit state to go anywhere.'

'I'm surprised, after all you called me yesterday—deceitful, lying, naïve—' she took a warped pleasure in reminding him equally '—that you should even care.'

'Of course I care.'

A glimmer of something deep inside her responded too eagerly to that heavily breathed statement. A throwback to her teenage years. That was all it was, she told herself chaotically.

'You're under my roof,' he went on, surprising her because she'd thought it was Mitch's house. 'I wouldn't want to be responsible for driving you out.'

'Your roof?' she enquired obliquely, while reluctantly processing the fact of his merely feeling responsible for her.

'Does that surprise you?'

'No.' Nothing about him surprised her.

'My roof. My house…' her breath caught sharply as the mattress suddenly depressed beneath his weight '…and my bed.'

His voice was arousing in itself, even without the things he was saying, and she thought of those couple of lovelorn weeks she had spent in his office, listening to his voice from behind that glass partition, wondering what it would be like to hear it roughened by desire.

'If Hélène's getting breakfast, we don't have time,' she said breathlessly because he was already turning back the sheet, making her whole body scream in anticipation.

He laughed softly. 'Oh, yes,' he said, pressing his lips against her forehead, and his voice was so soft she had to close her eyes because she couldn't deal with the depth of feeling it aroused in her, 'I think we do.'

CHAPTER EIGHT

RAYNE decided she had to go and visit Mitch at the clinic as soon as possible, since it had all come out now, who she was and why she was there.

She didn't feel like seeing a man who had used the terms of a signed agreement as a payback to ruin his ex-partner because, no matter how bad or naïve a businessman Grant Hardwicke had been, that was what Mitch had effectively done. But although she was still in shock over the things King had told her about her father, she still felt she owed it to Grant Hardwicke to hear the facts first-hand from Mitch himself.

At King's insistence, Rayne allowed him to drive her to the hospital, where a handful of reporters who had learned of Mitch's condition leaped on them like locusts as soon as they arrived at the main doors.

'Is it true, Mr Clayborne, that this health scare of your father's is more serious than the clinic is saying?'

'Is there any improvement in his condition?'

'Does this mean Clayborne shares in all areas are set to rise further with the expectation of your taking outright control?'

Questions came thick and fast, with microphones being thrust towards them, so that Rayne realised just how influential and newsworthy the Clayborne name was.

'You've heard the clinic spokesman's statement. My father's condition is stable,' King answered, pressing forward unperturbed, taking it in his stride. 'I've nothing more to add.'

'Mr Clayborne!' a female journalist shouted over the jostling heads. 'Can we deduce from your arriving here accompanied this morning...' her gossip-hungry gaze fell pointedly on Rayne '...that your relationship with super-model Sophie Ringwood is well and truly over?'

Rayne gave a small gasp as a flashbulb suddenly went off in her face.

'No comment,' King said, his arm coming instinctively around her.

Rayne was glad of his shielding strength, turning her head into the immaculate pale jacket covering his shoulder as the camera flashed again before he hustled her inside the building.

'I'm sorry about that.' His face was grim as they came into the bright modern efficiency of the airy clinic. 'It comes with the territory, I'm afraid.'

'Naturally,' Rayne returned, breathless from all the commotion, feeling the sudden loss of his arm around her shoulders. She didn't think she could ever get used to living life in the spotlight as he obviously had, she thought, trying not to dwell on what that reporter had said about his super-model girlfriend as he guided her towards a waiting lift.

'Remember he's ill,' King warned when she refused his offer to accompany her into Mitch's room as they were stepping out of the lift, insisting on going in alone. 'And it won't do either of you any good to get into a stew.'

'As if I would!' she breathed. 'Unlike your father, I do have ethics,' she added under her breath as a passing nurse, looking interestedly at King, gave Rayne the remainder of her smile.

The stark reminder of just how attractive he was to the opposite sex, coupled with nerves over how she was going to broach the subject with Mitch, made her look flushed and uneasy as she steeled herself to enter the man's room.

It was light and beautifully furnished, with only the bleep of a machine and other necessary equipment around the bed where Mitch was lying, propped up by pillows, reminding her that this wasn't some luxury hotel.

'How are you?' she asked with genuine concern, despite everything. He looked less florid and much more relaxed than she'd seen him before.

'No need for preliminaries, child.' Still his impatient self, he was waving her concern aside. 'You can see how I am. Alive! And you, I believe,' he went on, his watery blue eyes unsettlingly direct, 'have something you want to say to me.'

'All right, then.' Now she wondered why she had been worrying about exactly what she was going to say, but she should have known how much he was like King. Love them or hate them, the Clayborne men always made things easy by cutting to the chase. Always taking command. Well, like it or not. She could do that too! 'Why did you do what you did to my father?' she demanded with her breasts lifting rapidly under the light fabric of her flattering yet simply tailored shift. 'I don't care how many agreements he signed. You could have acknowledged that MiracleMed was his concept and you didn't.'

Mitch's mouth twisted as though he was considering how best to answer. 'Did King tell you that?' he enquired. 'That I could have done the decent thing and decided not to?'

'No. He didn't have to,' she murmured torturously, guessing that Mitch must have told him that yesterday, which was why King had looked so...what was it?...devastated, almost, she decided, when he had returned from here last night. But he hadn't told her because, of course, he would have wanted to protect his father, even though deep down he must have been shocked and thoroughly appalled. She didn't know how she knew that. She just did.

'Oh, I know about your...wife.' It hurt excruciatingly to say it. To have to accept that her father had been having an affair. 'And yes, King did tell me that. But surely that wasn't enough reason to…' She couldn't go on. Pain and resentment, anger and betrayal—it was all there in the anguish marring her face.

'Have you ever been in love, Rayne?' The man's tone had softened as his silver head tilted to study her. 'No, don't answer that.' His breath seemed dragged from him. 'That wasn't any excuse. But Karen was the only woman I'd loved since King's mother deserted me—deserted both of us—for an Australian rancher. I couldn't bear it when I saw the whole thing happening again. I was demented with anger—and jealousy.' His voice sounded even more gravelly than usual from his emotion. 'I figured that Grant had stolen from me—and something that no amount of money could buy—although I've realised since that I was half-crazed and too dim to see that she'd only married me for my money. I thought I was justified in taking something that belonged to him, but it's haunted me all these years in having done that to a colleague and a friend and, for what it's worth, I am truly, truly sorry.'

Feeling rooted to the spot, Rayne didn't know what to think—to say. What could she say? she demanded of herself, hurting unbearably.

With tears burning her eyes, her emotions riding high, she did the only thing she could.

She fled.

Only to bump into something warm and solid as she rounded the corner at the end of the corridor.

'What the…?'

King's hands were steadying her, his eyes scrutinizing her face and, seeing the tension and the tears she was battling to control, he said merely, understandingly, 'Come on.'

They were out of the building before she had even realised it.

The reporters were still there, eager for news of a budding romance.

King, however, shouldered his way through them, ignoring their intrusive questions until, finally, and much to Rayne's relief, he brought her—unmolested, but feeling the worse for wear—back to the car.

'Would you care to tell me about it?' he invited when they were on the road again in the exclusive, quiet haven of the Lamborghini.

'No,' was all she said.

To her relief, he didn't press the point. Silently, she thanked him for that.

Maybe in time she would forgive Mitchell Clayborne, she thought, sinking against the luxuriously padded pale leather upholstery. And even forgive her father. But right then all she could do was sit there with the sun filtering through the tinted windscreen, staring sightlessly out at the palm-fringed road and the glittering waves of a teal blue sea, wishing she had never come to Monte Carlo, wishing she could simply escape.

And perhaps King was wise to exactly how she was feeling, she speculated, surprised when, without a word, he took her for a long drive along the dramatically sculpted coast.

Above them, pastel-coloured houses seemed in places to cling precariously to cliff ledges among the forested mountains, while parasol pines, their branches spread with welcoming shade, grew abundantly amidst fig and date palms, interspersed with vibrant splashes of colour from the Mediterranean flowers.

She was beginning to feel better by the time he pulled onto the harbourside of an ancient port lined with a mixture of fishing boats and dinghies and exclusive yachts. A row of craft shops, galleries and cafés had been converted out of the old buildings beside the quay.

'Watch your footing,' he cautioned when they were out of the car, taking her hand to guide her safely past tethered ropes and crates of provisions being loaded onto vessels that amazed her with their sheer size. But it was those cool fingers around hers that left her breathless, with a sharp thrill running through her as she thought of the passion they had shared both that morning and the previous night.

His yacht was moored at one end of the ancient harbour and, after he had settled Rayne on board, leaving her brewing coffee in the well-equipped galley, King popped back to the quayside shops for some provisions.

The coffee had just brewed when Rayne heard him step back on board.

She was reaching up for two mugs in one of the modern cupboards just as he came down into the galley. His arm going around her waist made her gasp, as did the arrangement of white perfumed blooms he was holding against her breast and which were filling the air with their heady fragrance.

'Roses!' She laughed in breathless surprise.

'A peace offering,' King told her, 'for being such an overbearing oaf—and for jumping to all the wrong conclusions.' And when she looked enquiringly over her shoulder with a velvety eyebrow raised, he said, 'Mitch's previous record with a woman young enough to be his daughter resulted in devastating consequences. You couldn't blame me for being on my guard.'

'On your guard?' She gave a censorious little laugh. 'You've been like a prowling tiger!'

'Because I knew you were hiding something,' he said. 'You confirmed that the first morning when you said Mitch had told you I was in New York, because Mitch hadn't known. But also, I suspect, because I wanted—' He broke off, exhaling heavily as he pulled her back against him. 'Correction. Want you myself.'

Want. Nothing else, Rayne forewarned herself as every nerve leapt in response to the lips that were suddenly caressing the sensitive skin exposed to him by the slashed neckline of her simple shift.

'I just didn't want to be turned out before I was able to speak to Mitch. That's why I didn't tell the truth,' she murmured with a sensuous little shudder because of what he was doing to her.

'If you'd come to me—explained how you felt—I'd have at least looked into it,' he told her softly against her cheek now. 'Instead, I was left to pre-judge.'

'Without knowing anything about me,' she scolded gently. 'And you still don't know anything about me. Or very little,' she tagged on, with colour appearing along the crest of her cheekbones as she reminded herself that after last night and this morning, physically, at least, he knew her very, very well.

'Don't I?' He was smiling as though hugging some secret he wasn't prepared to share with her. Or perhaps, she thought, he was just remembering their time in bed together too...

'All right, so I rip men's shirts off and then take advantage of them when I've got them at their most vulnerable,' she conceded jokingly, loving the heat of his hand through the fine fabric of her dress and the warm strength of him pressing into her back.

Seriously, though, she couldn't help thinking about how shattered he had looked when he had returned from the clinic last night, after what had been an obviously gruelling day. Shattered, not just from worrying about Mitch, but by the things Mitch must have told him. Realising he'd been wrong about her, too, probably hadn't helped lessen the load.

'If that was taking advantage of me, then I can't wait for the next time,' he drawled, and pretended to double up when she gave him a gentle nudge in the ribs with her elbow.

'You're right. Enough of this or we'll starve,' he said, laughing, as she took the flowers and stood them in the centre of the dining table that curved around its seating area next to the galley. 'And then I do have an hour or so's work to do,' he apologised. 'But first...'

She hadn't realised it until then, but in his other hand he had been clutching the strap of a square insulated cooler, which he lifted up now onto the counter beside the cooker.

'Oysters in Madeira with cheese sauce for starters,' he told her, opening the bag and looking very pleased with himself. 'Fresh tuna steak—to be seared, of course—with salad and crusty bread and fresh raspberries and passion fruit coulis to follow.'

'Goodness!' Rayne laughed, realising she'd been expecting something far less exotic. 'When you go to town—you go to *town*!'

But of course he would, she thought, watching those long deft hands unpacking the carefully selected items. A man like Kingsley Clayborne would never do things by half measures.

'Oysters *and* passion fruit? Aren't oysters supposed to be an aphrodisiac?' she remembered with a sidelong provocative glance up at him. 'As for passion fruit…what sort of afternoon are you planning?'

'If you keep looking at me like that, not a very productive one,' he responded with a feral smile.

'And don't tell me…' she laughed again, thinking how wonderful it was to feel so at ease with him '…Clayborne's shares will drop like a stone and the whole global workforce will be on the dole because the company's CEO stopped to enjoy himself for a while.'

'That's about the size of it,' he replied dryly, although there was a hint of seriousness in his voice that made her realise how hard he worked and how dedicated he was in what he did, which helped provide a living for so many thousands of people across the globe.

'So how did you come by all this stuff for such a gourmet meal?' Rayne asked. After all, he hadn't been gone *that* long.

'The owner of that restaurant over there…' this with a sideways toss of his head towards the quayside '…is a very good friend of mine. I rang him earlier and told him to expect me.'

'You…' *dark horse*, she finished silently, warmed by the knowledge that he'd been planning all this even before they had left the clinic. Probably even the roses too.

She couldn't remember much of what they talked about during the meal, which they ate out on the lower deck under the awning. Their conversation was light and casual and surprisingly easy. Then afterwards, with the dishwasher humming away in the galley and King working in the salon on his laptop, she lazed on the upper deck in her burgundy satin bra and panties because she didn't have her bikini with her.

Listening to the deep resonance of his voice, hanging on every word he uttered as he conducted his international business over the phone and arranged meetings, her gently tanning body pulsed from the memory of their lovemaking, and throbbed in reckless anticipation of what might be to come.

Her cellphone rang while she was lying there. She didn't recognise the caller as anyone she knew, answering it rather uncertainly.

'Hello, Lorrayne,' Nelson Faraday began. 'I got your number from an old associate of ours...' He named a mutual colleague with whom they had worked on the same paper and with whom Rayne still sometimes kept in touch. 'He told me your mother had been ill. I hope she's feeling better.' Preliminaries over with, he dived straight into the reason why he was ringing her. 'I understand you were seen looking more than chummy with Kingsley Clayborne. Want to tell me about it?'

A trickle of unease ran through Rayne like a paralysing poison. 'No.'

'Just good friends, eh? Or is there far more to your being here with him than meets the eye?'

'I don't know what you're talking about,' she said tremulously, knowing this man could spell trouble for her.

The journalist chuckled softly, without a trace of humour. 'Don't you? You have a short memory, Lorrayne.'

'If you think I've forgotten the methods you use to dig up your stories, then trust me—my memory's as long as an elephant's!'

Laughter came again, a little more sincerely now. 'That sounds more like the fiery creature I knew. Look, I think we should talk. How about meeting me for drinks at the Café de Paris?'

The man had to be joking! 'How about barking up some other tree, Faraday? I've got nothing to say to you. Goodbye!'

She found she was shaking as she cut him off and tossed down her phone on the sunbed.

'What's wrong?' King asked, choosing that exact moment to emerge from the lower deck.

His shirt was partially unbuttoned with the sleeves rolled up to the elbows, and with those light beige trousers moulding themselves to his hips and very muscular thighs he looked no less than utterly magnificent.

'Nothing,' Rayne fibbed, trying to restore her agitated features into some semblance of order.

'Nothing?' He glanced down at her cellphone, dark brows knitting together. Numbly, she wondered exactly what she might have said and how much he might have heard.

'Just someone ringing up enquiring about Mum,' she supplied, which was partly true at any rate. She even managed a smile.

'She's all right, isn't she?'

The concern lining his face with that strong hand on her shoulder had the effect of melting her worries like butter over a hot stove.

'Of course,' she murmured, tilting her head back, her smile genuine this time, her peach-tinted lips inviting—craving— the pressure of his.

'Do you think if I kiss you I'll be able to finish what I'm doing down there?' he suggested dryly, touching a finger to his lips and pressing that to her yearning mouth instead.

Sensations ignited in her like a bush-fire even from that simple gesture from him as he handed her one of his clean white shirts.

'You've had enough sun for one day,' he remarked solicitously, doing nothing to quell the fire raging inside her as his fingers brushed her sun-warmed shoulder. 'Put it on.'

She obeyed as he disappeared below. She'd been thinking of going inside anyway, but she'd been too ensnared by some kind of sensual torpor from imagining doing all sorts of delectable things with him to move.

Perhaps it was true. Perhaps oysters *were* an aphrodisiac, she thought, lounging back and putting Nelson Faraday from her mind. Or perhaps it was just the warmth of the sun on her body. Even so, just the sight of King had rekindled all the outrageously sensual things she had been thinking about him before her cellphone rang, so that it was twenty minutes or so before, aching for his company, she picked up her bag and phone and the suncream she'd found in the shower room and went below.

Now, as she stepped down into the air-conditioned comfort of the salon, she saw him lounging back on the luxuriously padded sofa, having just closed his laptop for the day. There was music coming from the hi-fi system, which was in fact what had brought her in. A plaintive, achingly beautiful melody that was as familiar to her as it was moving.

'The New World Symphony,' she identified, smiling broadly. 'I love this piece!'

'I know.'

'What?' She looked down at him quizzically. 'How can you?'

'Because I just happened to be there the morning your father came into the office and said you'd bought this CD with some birthday money you'd been given and that he was glad to get back to work as you'd been playing it non-stop all that weekend.'

'And you remembered that?' Rayne marvelled with an amazed little laugh. After all, it was seven years ago!

'Only because I recall thinking that it wasn't the type

of music I associated with the half-scarecrow, half-vampire image,' he drawled.

Rayne laughed again. 'Was I really that bad?'

'You were really that bad,' he admitted, his mouth moving wryly. Yet, strangely, there had been something about her willowy shape behind that glass partition during her short spell in that office that had acted like a magnet on his eyes.

'I was also a beanpole,' she remembered. Underdeveloped and rake-thin from always being on an unnecessary diet. 'No wonder you ignored me!' And she'd thought she looked so lovely, she remembered self-mockingly. If only she'd known! 'You weren't averse to my music, though, were you?' she reminded him coquettishly, with a toss of her head towards the music system. Then, with a soft pout to her mouth, 'Even if you would have preferred to spank me than to take me out.'

His lips twisted in mocking censure of what he had said the previous night.

'I couldn't be,' he responded, and smiled then, so warmly it made her heart miss a beat. 'It's a personal favourite of mine too.'

For some reason that pleased her more than anything else he could have said. It meant that he shared her taste, created a mutual rapport between them.

'I read that the composer was trying to convey a feeling of homesickness in this part,' she remembered aloud as the music swelled poignantly through the luxurious vessel. 'It's supposed to be about someone who'd gone to America looking for a better life, looking out at unfamiliar mountains and longing for home.'

'Quite possibly,' King agreed. 'I believe Dvořák wrote it while he was in New York—himself a stranger, many, many miles from home.'

'I didn't know that.' There was something so pleasurable in talking with him like this after all the animosity there had been between them. 'Don't you think the feeling comes over well?'

He nodded and said, 'Brilliantly.'

'So what does it make *you* think about?' she pressed, unable to imagine a man like him romanticising and going off into some dreamy fantasy world like she had whenever she had played it.

Pursing his lips, King dragged his gaze from the two scraps of burgundy lace beneath the gaping shirt—which looked a hell of a lot better on her than it did on him, he decided—before considering her question.

Quite simply that music always reminded him of his mother. It had been her favourite piece, too. Her albums were just some of the many personal things she had left behind when she had walked out that day, what seemed a lifetime ago, never to return.

He'd been five years old and nursing homesickness so acute he'd thought he'd die from the ache inside him. Because that was how it had felt when she had left. As if she'd ripped out his heart and taken it with her, or as if someone had robbed him of his home. He remembered standing at the window, day after day, with Mitch constantly playing and replaying that music, waiting for her to turn the corner of the street as if she had just been to the shops, waiting for her familiar smile, her wave—waiting for her to come home.

But Rayne had asked him what it made him think about and he had to give her an answer.

'Things I couldn't have,' he replied heavily, but honestly now.

The rawness in his voice had Rayne searching his face for any clue to his emotions as he leaned back against the cushions, staring out of the oblong window at the sun-streaked water. He looked so distant and so bleak that she wanted to stretch out a hand and touch his cheek, ease the loneliness she sensed lay hidden inside him, buried in a place too deep for her to reach.

'What sort of things?' she whispered, wise enough to realise that he wasn't talking about anything that money or influence or power could buy.

He smiled then, giving her his full attention, shrugging off what she knew was a moment of regretted weakness.

'Never you mind,' he dismissed lightly. 'So what about you?' he prompted from behind that impervious shell of his, although the teasing crept back into his voice as he continued, 'What did you dream about when you drove your family and friends—and probably the whole neighbourhood,' he said with a grimace, 'mad with Dvořák's New World Symphony?'

You.

She couldn't say it as she met those steel-blue eyes. Couldn't tell him that she used to imagine him sweeping her up in his arms one day when she had pretended to lose her way and wandered deliberately into his office. Imagined him carrying her off to a luxurious bed somewhere where he would slowly undress her, kissing and stroking each area of sensitive flesh he had uncovered. And all the time this music would be playing, its swelling crescendo the moment he made her his, with his deep voice whispering between kisses the one thing she craved to hear him say.

I love you.

From her wild imaginings, those three words suddenly took on a startlingly new meaning, coming as they did from the depth of her own feelings and shocking her with their intensity.

I love him, she thought, *which is why I never stopped hurting when I believed how much he had hurt Dad. I've always loved him! I love him now! And I always will!*

The feeling swelled and grew, the realisation of how little she knew about him, not to mention for how short a time, not mattering one iota. She'd been made for him and she had known it from the second she had first laid eyes on him all those years ago.

The knowledge held her rigid, every second that she stayed conveying to him how hopelessly ensnared she was, but she couldn't move or tear her gaze from the mesmerising depths of his.

She knew what a temptation she must look with the shirt he'd lent her hanging open and revealing her scanty underwear. And she knew he obviously thought so too when his mouth compressed with some inner satisfaction as he allowed himself a visual journey of her rapidly rising breasts to the dark triangle of satin at the juncture of her thighs, his eyes flickering with masculine appreciation beneath the dark sweep of his lashes.

'Come here,' he commanded softly.

The next second he had caught her hand and electrifying sensations ripped through her as he tipped her off balance, tugging her down across his lap.

'What are you doing?' she gasped, pretending to look shocked, wild impulses crackling through every nerve-ending from the heat that was pulsing through her veins.

'You accused me of not giving you any attention in the past,' he proclaimed, his mouth set with exciting purpose. 'I wouldn't want you thinking I was holding out on you now.'

Galvanized by his actions and by the excitement that was licking through her blood, Rayne clutched him to her with a throaty sob of pleasure as their mouths met and his hand found the eager heat of her body beneath the open shirt, massaging and moulding as it moved over her waist, along her ribcage, up and up until it found her straining breasts.

The satin cups were a hindrance to him—to them both—and, sliding a finger inside, he pulled each one down in turn to expose her breasts to his fervid gaze, accentuating their aching fullness.

She let out a shuddering gasp when he ran his hand across

them and watched the way her eyes darkened with desire as he caressed each warm mound in turn.

She had always wished her breasts were smaller, but she didn't any more. She was suddenly proud of her voluptuous curves, knowing they emphasised her femininity, proud of the pleasure she was giving King as well as receiving in turn as he lifted her eager body to taste each tingling crest with a circling tongue.

'Not bad for a beanpole,' he murmured teasingly.

Twisting around so that he was half lying on top of her, his lips were suddenly following his hands on a path of sweet torture along her body, driving her crazy for him, bending her to his will.

She murmured her pleasure, arching her body in involuntary response. But there was something she needed from him before she let this happen again. Something she needed to know...

'What about...'

She couldn't say it at first, her silence bringing his dark head up for a second from somewhere around her middle.

'What about what?' he prompted, his lips over her midriff refusing to be stilled.

'Sophie Ringwood.'

'What about her?'

'Are you still involved with her?' she uttered on a shuddering breath because he'd moved back along her body and his hands were making possessive claim to her breasts once more.

'No. It was over between us months ago,' he murmured, his warm breath on the inner edge of her ear driving her crazy, even though she needed to be serious for a few moments, to stay in control.

'The press didn't seem to think so.'

'The press just sensationalize to sell newspapers,' he breathed along the perfumed column of her throat. 'Surely you know that.'

'True,' she admitted in a voice almost strangled from the pleasure of what he was doing to her. 'But I also believe that there's never smoke without fire.'

Her persistence dragged him back from his sensational exploration of her body, compelling him to sit up and take notice of what she was saying. His features were flushed from his arousal and he was breathing heavily. 'Then you'll just have to trust me when I say that, much as the media like to make a song and dance about every woman I'm seen with, I've always thought it less than politic to involve myself with more than one woman at a time.'

He was trailing his fingers along her inner thigh, seeking access to that most secret part of her that was aching for his touch. But suddenly she clamped her legs together, trapping his hand between them as she asked the question which seemed ludicrous in the circumstances, but which she needed to ask.

'Are you saying *we're* involved?'

His irises were darkened with desire as he gazed sombrely down at her where she lay draped over his arm, but something flared in their depths beneath his heavily lidded eyes.

'Don't you think lying here naked in my arms constitutes an involvement?' he put to her incredulously. 'And that this...' a low, almost agonised moan escaped her as his probing fingers sought and found the wet warmth of her femininity '...marks us as lovers?' he suggested, sounding unashamedly possessive. 'Unless there's something you're not telling me. Like you have a boyfriend back home in England—and then I think I really *will* turn you over my knee.'

He wouldn't, of course. Intuition alone told her that. There was a reckless excitement, though, in knowing he had said it simply because he wanted her for himself.

He might have known quite a few women intimately, if the papers were to be believed. But he obviously abhorred cheating in a relationship—which was why he'd sounded so unforgiving last night towards Grant Hardwicke and his step-mother, she realised, loving him for his morals and how principled he was, hardly daring to hope that she might have some sort of future with him.

Would he fall in love with her? Eventually? Decide that he'd had enough of top models and actresses and hard-nosed, beautiful businesswomen and settle for someone who wasn't always vying for position with him and getting her name in the papers?

But she didn't want to think about that because that was getting too far ahead of herself. And, anyway, she couldn't think about anything else because his long practised fingers were working their magic and driving her crazy for him.

There was something incredibly erotic in what he was doing to her, she realised, feeling like a puppet being worked by her puppeteer. He was in control and all that was required of her was to do his bidding, which right now was to writhe against him and show him just how much pleasure he was giving her.

With her nails sinking into his arm, she clutched at him like someone drowning, sobbing and bucking as the sensually induced rhythm sent breath-quickening tingles licking along her thighs.

She had never felt so abandoned or so ungoverned as she did at that moment when, with one last thrust of her hips towards his deeply penetrating fingers, she climaxed and collapsed against him, sobbing and gasping, while he cupped her femininity and held her until the tensions throbbed out of her body.

CHAPTER NINE

KING awoke and reached automatically for the woman lying in the big bed beside him.

Rayne was still sleeping peacefully, with her slender body turned towards him, and for a few moments he lay simply watching her, his hand still, yet resting possessively on the gentle curve of her hip.

He had made love to her almost endlessly since that first time, two nights ago, when he had come back from the clinic, having realised he had been wrong about her—that she wasn't a gold-digger, out for her own ends—having already discovered who she was.

He marvelled now at how he hadn't recognised her earlier. Or perhaps he had—subconsciously—he thought in retrospect. Perhaps that was why she'd got under his skin from that very first evening he had come back here and seen her standing out there on the terrace. Perhaps a part of him had been yielding to a long-lost attraction that had ended before it had even begun, although he'd never have acknowledged it then. At twenty-three he had been too busy getting his life mapped out—dating women closer to his own age, who promised to fulfil a part of him that could never be fulfilled—to really notice Lorri Hardwicke. But after she had gone he'd missed her, he realised now. Missed the way she'd looked at him like an adoring young fawn whenever he spoke to her, missed her smile, her quiet presence. Though he would never have consciously acknowledged that either, seven years ago, he thought with a self-deprecating smile.

She stirred for a moment, snuggling closer to him, and he waited for her to open her eyes, but she didn't. Her mouth was curved slightly as though whatever she was dreaming about pleased her, and he couldn't help hoping that it was him.

She was warm and gentle and caring. He already knew that from the past. And whatever she had done to get herself into Mitch's—and consequently *his*—life, she had done only with her father's interests at heart. In fact, he found himself admiring the drive and spirit it must have taken to motivate her to act in such a way—to even think about taking on someone as intimidating and hard-bitten as Mitch.

'I've lost her, King,' he'd lamented when King, after driving Rayne back from the yacht last night, had made a flying visit to the clinic to check on his father's condition—which he'd been grateful to learn was improving—and Mitch had told him what had transpired between him and Rayne earlier in the day. 'Lost any respect she might have had for me—or what I thought she had for me,' he'd corrected with a grimace, 'when I didn't know who she was. Can you persuade her not to think too badly of me?' he'd appealed to King. 'I was a mad fool—in love—when I did what I did. But what's the point of telling that to you? I can't expect you—least of anyone—to imagine what that's like, can I?'

No, he couldn't, King thought now, because he'd never been in love. And his father knew it. Knew better than anyone how he had learned from childhood—and in the cruellest way possible—the folly that lay in putting his trust in a woman. And neither Mitch's second marriage nor any of his own cautious relationships had changed his views on that.

That didn't stop him wanting, however. And since Lorrayne Hardwicke had unintentionally stepped into his life last week he'd been almost permanently aroused.

Just like now, he thought wryly as he lay there, hot and

hard, studying the gentle curvature of her face, framed by that wild mass of red hair, finding himself unable to stop thinking of all they had done and what he still wanted to do to her.

Do with her, he amended shamefully, because he wanted her with him for more than just good sex. He wanted to take her places, and not just to show her off as the Sophie Ringwoods of this world always wanted him to do, but to keep her all for himself. Show her new things and experiences she might be interested in and that they could discuss together—for however long it might last—while he discovered everything he didn't already know about her. Which surely made her a pretty high contender on his list of special women, he realised, of which there had been only one or two in his adult life. And, as he still couldn't deny, the sex was pretty good. In fact it was more than that. It was sensational.

It didn't help cool his libido in any way to remember the way she had been with him yesterday. As if she had been on that yacht solely to give him pleasure…like when he had brought her to orgasm that first time and her wild response to him had made him feel like a billion dollars. And afterwards, when he had suggested that they go to bed, she had undressed him slowly and provocatively, caressing and adoring his body as if it were a temple, using her lips and hands and finally her soft mouth…

Feeling he was going to explode if he didn't do something to temper his urges, he slid out of bed and abandoned all thought of waking her for the invigorating effects of a cold shower.

Rayne awoke to see the sun blazing around the edges of the blind, a fierce Mediterranean sun that regained its strength so early each day that it could have been seven a.m. or noon.

The other side of the bed was empty, she discovered, rolling on to her side, only the rumpled sheet with the imprint of King's head on the adjoining pillow assuring her that she hadn't dreamed the smile-inducing pleasures of the previous night.

She felt like someone who had died from too much loving and gone to heaven, remembering how King had made himself master of her body, time after glorious time and time again.

But it wasn't just that that had her spirits soaring this morning. It was because of knowing how compatible they were, as well as discovering that vulnerable side to King—not only over the past few days, but particularly yesterday—and the secret pleasure of having realised just how much she loved him.

She knew he had been scarred quite badly. It must have been excruciating as a small boy to be deserted like that by his own mother, she sympathised, and then not to have had a close relationship with Mitch. It was no wonder he had turned out so hard-bitten and self-sufficient, evident from the way he hadn't yet loved anyone enough to settle down. Hadn't taken on the role of husband and father and got himself involved in the joys and sorrows of having children of his own. But instinctively she knew that deep down he was a very lonely man, and that she could change all that if he would only let her. And to do that she had to convince him of how deeply he could trust her—convince herself that one day she could make him fall in love with her...

Having showered and dressed in lemon shorts and a lemon and white T-shirt, Rayne found King in the study, browsing through some paperwork by the filing cabinet.

'Ah, there you are!' he said, the smile he gave her heating her blood from the hair she'd twisted loosely on top of her head to her softly golden feet in her Indian flip-flops. 'I thought I was going to have to come up and tickle those delightfully painted toes.'

'Why didn't you?' she crooned provocatively, sidling up to him and inhaling the tantalising scent of his cologne, which emanated from beneath the white T-shirt stretched across his

wide muscular chest. He'd teamed it with pale lightweight
trousers that hugged his powerful hips and legs and the whole
image emphasised his fitness and hard virility.

'Because if I had I wouldn't have stopped with just your
toes,' he admitted with a wry tug of his mouth. 'And where
do you think we would be now?'

In paradise, Rayne thought with a secretive little smile but,
running idle fingers down the exciting contours of his arm,
she murmured, 'It *is* only seven o'clock.'

He checked his watch, which was gleaming gold against
the black strap spanning his wrist. 'And have you any idea
how long we were in bed?'

Not long enough, she thought, wondering how, after all
their hours of lovemaking, she could want him with an almost insatiable hunger that was still demanding to be fed.

'I had a rough night. I needed my beauty sleep,' she declared with a mischievous twinkle in her eyes.

'No, you didn't.' He folded her gently into his arms, pressing his lips against the ridge of her nose. 'You're beautiful
enough,' he breathed. 'As for rough…' He chuckled softly.
'I wasn't aware of hearing any complaints on that score last
night.'

Because he was a consummate lover, Rayne marvelled,
being as exquisitely tender as he was passionate.

'Then shut up and kiss me,' she ordered playfully, thinking she'd die of wanting if he didn't hurry up and do so.
'Otherwise I might—'

As his mouth swooped down over hers, cutting her off
in full flow, suddenly he was the one taking command. She
felt the surge of his body as he pulled her hard against him,
thrilling her with the knowledge that she could have this effect on such an incredible man.

'I think,' he rasped, coming up for air, 'that I'm going to
have to take you out for breakfast. Otherwise, we're just going
to wind up back in bed. And, much as I'd welcome that diver-

sion right now, there are a number of administrative things that require my attention before the day's out.'

'Is there anything I can help you with?' she volunteered, wanting as much as she wanted his lovemaking to be useful to him.

'You? Help?' He looked both surprised and amused.

'Why not?' she suggested. 'I type. I can do your letters for you. I'll even edit them if you want me to.'

Of course, King thought, smiling reflectively. She was a journalist, which required using all her powers of initiative. Even so, he was touched by her desire to help him, especially on a beautiful day like this. Most women he'd known—particularly Sophie Ringwood—used to complain that he was always working and that he wasn't giving them enough attention. This woman, however—despite how pig-headedly he had treated her to start with—was offering him her time and effort and her intellectual skills, not just the generosity of her beautiful body.

'If you could, it would cut the time in half,' he said. 'And then I'm yours for the rest of the day.'

A little frisson ran through Rayne, not just from the thought of helping him, but also from what he'd said about being hers.

'Promise,' she purred, touching her tongue alluringly to her top lip, and though she knew he'd meant having him sexually, her heart wanted to interpret it as much more than that.

There was a warming satisfaction in sharing the more serious aspects of his life with him, Rayne decided a little later, hugging the feeling to her as she filed a copy of the letter she had recently typed for him just as he finished making some highly important international call.

'Whoever put this away put it in the wrong file,' she observed, waving the errant copy letter she had just removed from its clip over her shoulder.

'Thanks for noticing. It was probably me,' King remarked,

coming across to the filing cabinet to take it from her, and she guessed that even if it hadn't been his own mistake, he wasn't the type of man who would openly blame his secretary in front of anyone else.

Impressed with her efficiency, taking the letter from her, King stooped to press his lips to the inviting nape of her beautifully exposed neck, feeling his urges rising almost instantly.

She was clearly bra-less beneath her top, and the warmth of her, with that faintly exotic perfume, was driving him just short of insane.

'Do you usually do this to all your secretaries?' she asked with a delicious little shiver when his arm, coming diagonally across her breasts, drew her back against him so that she could feel the potent warmth of his superbly masculine body.

'No,' he responded deeply. 'Nor have I ever made love to one on my desk before.'

'You're not!' she squealed excitedly, her breath shortening because he'd swung her up into his arms and was striding back with her across the room, before stooping to sweep papers aside with a careless arm and setting her down on the hard green leather surface. 'Someone might come in! One of the maids. Hélène...'

'To hell with Hélène and the maids,' he ground out through a jaw clenched rigid with sexual tension. 'To hell with work, with business and the whole darn world!' Because that was how she made him feel.

Heat radiated through Rayne's blood as he leaned across her, taking her mouth and reaching up to tug the pins out of her hair.

'That's better,' he approved breathlessly, his eyes burning with feverish satisfaction as the fiery swathe tumbled wildly about her shoulders. 'That's how I like you. Looking hot and dishevelled. Like you've just spent all night in my bed.'

But there was more to this, he thought. Much more than this. She had the power to make him lose control like no other woman had ever been able to do—the power to make him feel things that he had never allowed himself to feel. He didn't know where it could lead—or how. He only knew that over the past few days he had allowed her to get under his well-protected skin and that she didn't look like surfacing from it at any time soon.

Nor did he want her to…

'Promise me you'll always be here when I need you like this,' he rasped, his sentence broken by the fevered kisses along her cheek, her throat, against her hair.

Was he proposing? Rayne's mind swam from the staggering possibility.

But no, he wasn't, her common sense quickly kicked in to assure her. He just wanted her in his bed, although instinct told her that he wasn't a man who would make a suggestion like that lightly.

I promise, she breathed silently, so close to agreeing to become his mistress that she wasn't sure how she would have answered if the intercom beside them hadn't buzzed—and kept on buzzing until King threw up a switch when it became clear that the person on the other end wasn't going to be ignored.

'Yes. What is it?' he demanded in a voice roughened by passion.

'There's a bunch of reporters outside the gates,' the voice of the English security guard Rayne had seen around the place announced, sounding particularly harassed.

'Have you told them my father's condition is stable? That he isn't giving them the satisfaction of dropping off the planet just to give them a story?' King's words were strung with impatience.

There was a fairly long pause before the other man said, 'I think it's more about you and Miss Hardwicke, sir.'

A rising tension started to grip Rayne before King swore under his breath and sat up.

'For heaven's sake, Peters! You've dealt with this sort of thing often enough to know what to do.'

'Yes, sir. But this is different. I think you'd better come down.'

'What is it?' Rayne asked nervously, the thought of having her affair with King reported by the press abhorrent to her. But a deep-buried fear—a fear that had surfaced when she'd seen Nelson Faraday here the other day and then spoken to him yesterday—made her stomach start to feel queasy and her mouth go dry.

'Welcome to the rich man's world, Rayne,' King muttered with a grimace. 'You'll get used to it, but it still doesn't make it acceptable or any less annoying.'

She had to admit he looked annoyed—very annoyed—as he got to his feet.

'I should have gone.' She didn't intend to say it, except that she had this feeling that her whole world was about to explode.

'No, you shouldn't.' King's brows were drawn together as he bent down and kissed the top of her head. 'Stay here,' he advised calmly, straightening his clothes and running hasty fingers through his hair because someone had started rapping on the door.

'Hélène?'

She looked as flustered as the morning she had come and told them that Mitch wasn't well, Rayne thought as King opened the door.

Already on her feet, Rayne felt the dubious glances the housekeeper was casting her way.

'It is this article, Monsieur King. In the English paper.'

Rayne could see that it was folded at a particular page as King took the newspaper from her.

'Mon dieu!'

'All right, Hélène. I'll deal with it.'

The housekeeper seemed on the verge of tears as King closed the door behind her.

'What the…?'

'What is it?' Rayne whispered, hardly daring to breathe, watching the strong masculine features that had been flushed from their lovemaking turn pale as he continued to read.

'Would you care to explain *this?*' he seethed when he'd finished, thrusting the newspaper at her.

Rayne's blood seemed to freeze in her veins as she recognised the photograph of herself and King and read the bold headline above it.

IN BED WITH THE ENEMY?

Her fingers were trembling so much she could scarcely clutch the page as her darting eyes digested what had been written about them.

It seems that this century's Captain of Commerce and Technology, Kingsley Clayborne, might have switched his allegiance from the sex kittens of screen and catwalk for the deadlier claws of the tabloid press.
Small-time journalist Lorrayne Hardwicke, seen here arriving at the hospital with Clayborne's illustrious CEO yesterday, is reported to have allegedly accused the corporate giant of purloining the software, MiracleMed, while her father was an employee with the firm.

To her horror, it went on to mention Grant Hardwicke and his exact position with the company.

If there is any truth in these rumours—and our undisclosed source suggests that there is—then what is the lovely twenty-five-year-old doing with King, anyway? Or does it, as this picture suggests, mean that

*all those allegations have been put to bed, because it
certainly looks as though these two have finally kissed
and made up?*

Rayne could only stare at the photograph of the two of
them together, which depicted her walking with her face
turned towards King, while he had a protective arm around
her shoulders, trying to shield her from the glare of the camera.

'I…I can't,' she stammered, shaking her head in disbelief.

'Oh, come on, Rayne!' King's anger was white-hot, barely
controlled. 'You can do better than that!'

'I can't! I didn't know anything about this!'

'Well, someone did! Who else would have known about
those allegations only forty-eight hours after I'd found out
the truth myself if you hadn't told them?'

The chill that had been gripping her spread slowly out-
wards from her heart to her very extremities. She knew
without even reading the by-line. It was the work of Nelson
Faraday!

Ice trickled through her veins as all her worst fears were
manifested in the article she was holding. It was what she had
been dreading ever since the morning she'd come down and
seen who King's interviewer was.

'What's the matter, darling?' There was no warmth in the
way he said it. 'Were you planning to be gone before this…'
he was snatching the paper from her '…this gutter-mongering
came out?'

'No!'

'Then can you look me in the eyes and tell me honestly
that you had nothing to do with this? That you never contacted or discussed the facts about your father and this company with Faraday?'

She wanted to say no. To sweep away the hurt, anger and

disbelief with which he was looking at her. But how could she? she asked herself, agonised.

Dropping her head into her hands with her loose hair tumbling around them, she just stood there and groaned.

'I see,' King rasped, and it was all there in his voice. Condemnation. Disillusionment. Disgust.

'No, you don't,' Rayne sighed, dragging her fingers down her face as she brought her head up in an all but vain attempt to change his harshening opinion of her.

'Then enlighten me, sweetheart.'

His false endearments and his cutting tone pierced her to the heart after all they had shared, and especially after his tenderness of only a few minutes ago. 'Tell me what bizarre coincidence has suddenly led to this article coming out if you're as innocent as you're trying to lead me to believe.'

She shook her head. 'The only coincidence is that he's here,' she murmured, remembering how sick to the stomach she had felt when she had seen him coming in that day with King from the terrace.

'So you thought you'd capitalise on your fortuitousness and get your story to him while he was still here.'

'No!'

'When exactly did you do it, Rayne? The day you saw him here? Yesterday? Wasn't it him you were speaking to on the boat when I came up on deck?'

'Yes, but—'

'So while we were making love and you were driving me insane by making me feel like I was the only man you ever wanted to be with, you'd already been up there playing both sides of the coin and plying him with…this!' The way he stabbed the newspaper with an angry finger made her visibly flinch.

'No. That isn't true!' she protested, hurting, unable to imagine how he could reduce something as incredible as what they had had on his boat yesterday afternoon to something so low.

'Really? Then tell me what is? Or would you actually know the truth if it hit you, Lorrayne?'

He couldn't believe he was standing here speaking to her like this. But then he hadn't reckoned on being played for such a fool. Neither had he reckoned on how close he had come to trusting her, or how much he had wanted to trust her. The fact that he couldn't was like a knife twisting inside him, gouging out scars that even a lifetime's immunity hadn't healed.

'I did tell him about MiracleMed,' she admitted shakily. 'But not yesterday. And not recently. It was years ago, when we worked together. And I did it without even thinking. I didn't know he'd ever use it in any way to hurt anyone. To hurt me... I was as naïve as they came. Dad was going through a bad time and drinking heavily. I just needed someone to talk to and...well...he was there.'

'And he just happened to resurrect all that? Risk a lawsuit over something someone of little more importance than the office junior told him goodness knows how many years ago?' He looked and sounded incredulous and, put like that, she could see why he didn't believe her.

'He came here. He saw me with you.' And suspected there was something amiss about her being here when he realised she wasn't using her real name.

'So?'

'It obviously jogged his memory.'

'Obviously!' King wasn't giving any quarter.

'And he's always been one to bear a grudge.'

'And why would he do that? Did you rob him of a story? Is that it?'

'No.'

'Then you'd better give me a reason, Rayne, and you'd better make it good!'

'Because I wouldn't sleep with him!' she hurled back, wounded by his inexorable interrogation. 'Satisfied?'

For a moment he just stood there, looking as though she had just taken the wind right out of his sails.

'You slept with me. The so-called "enemy",' he reminded her with disdain in the hard, twisting line of his mouth.

'That's different.'

'Why? Because I'm a much better proposition?' he suggested cruelly.

Because I love you! her mind screamed, although she couldn't tell him that.

'Believe that if you want to,' she murmured instead, feeling his contempt like an arrow piercing her heart. 'I've told you the truth. Why won't you believe me?' she appealed to him, and knew the answer even before he replied.

'Give me one good reason why I should.'

He was standing there with his fists balled against his hips, the offending crumpled newspaper still clutched in his hand.

Because it's the truth, she wanted to say again, but knew that it would be futile. She had deceived him in the beginning. By lying about her passport. Her reason for being there. By not coming clean about who she was.

'If you trusted me, I wouldn't have to,' she said resignedly, knowing she'd done nothing to earn that trust, nor would she ever be likely to. It was written all over his hard, handsome face, in the bleak, steely depths of his eyes.

She couldn't stay there and look at him any longer. She brushed past him and ran up to her room, where she collapsed on the bed in a state of total despair.

If she left now she would have to run the gauntlet of reporters, but even that was preferable to staying here and suffering the torture of King's contempt.

He didn't love her, and she'd been a fool to imagine that there could ever have been any chance of him loving her, she thought, castigating herself for being so stupid.

She'd been a fling. A way of distracting himself from everything else that had happened over the past week. But what she had thought had begun to grow between them would never have stood the test of time if what little respect and belief he had had in her could be pounded into the ground at the first hurdle.

She heard the growl of the Lamborghini as she was dragging her suitcase up onto the bed, rushing to the window in time to see it tearing down past the curve in the drive towards the electrically operated gates.

It didn't stop to appease the paparazzi who would have had to leap aside to let it pass, and her only thought, as she visualised the gates closing behind the powerful car and heard the sound of its throbbing engine roaring away, was that she would probably never see Kingsley Clayborne again.

CHAPTER TEN

PREGNANT? How could she be? Rayne asked herself over and over, as she had been doing since it had been confirmed over a week ago now.

She had been taking the Pill. A low dosage one, it was true. But she'd believed it to be a foolproof contraceptive. Apart from which, when she'd made love with King over those wild few days in Monaco, she'd felt an added security in the knowledge that it was probably the safest time of her cycle.

But Nature, it seemed, was mocking her in its triumph over seeing her impregnated with King Clayborne's seed. Against all the odds. Against their best intentions. And against—she was certain where King was concerned, anyway—his strongest wishes. She was only relieved that he wasn't around to find out.

Queasily, she wheeled her supermarket trolley to the checkout and started unloading its contents.

It had been over ten weeks since she had left the Monaco mansion, fleeing in a cab—doing as King had done and ignoring the paparazzi—intent only on getting the first flight home. Ten weeks since she had left a note for him, propped up on his bedside cabinet, to the effect that she'd been telling him the truth and wishing him well.

He hadn't responded. Nor had she expected him to. She was just a girl he had had a good time with, for as short a time as it had been doomed to last.

The press had hounded her for a couple of weeks, but when she refused to comment on the alleged accusations, or on her relationship with King, they had backed off and it had all blown over. Probably, she guessed, because she wasn't newsworthy enough to warrant any more attention, since it was obvious she wasn't one of his *favoured* women.

And now she was carrying his child. A child whose two grandfathers had wound up hating each other, and whose father certainly didn't have any love for its mother.

Inserting her credit card into the machine when the assistant gave her the total amount of her bill, Rayne felt the bite of anguished tears behind her eyes as she attempted to key in her pin number.

'Take it out and try again,' the checkout girl told her in a sing-song voice when the machine refused to accept the number she had given it.

She did, only to have the same thing happen again—twice.

She heard the girl muttering something about getting it authorised when a deep voice from the queue behind her suggested, 'Allow me.'

Rayne swung round and found herself looking up into the steely gaze of two heart-wrenchingly familiar blue eyes.

'King!' Every self-destructive nerve pulsed into life and everything else around her seemed to melt away, leaving her breathless from his tall, dark, imposing masculinity. 'You don't have to,' she uttered croakily, trembling so much she was hardly able to speak. But he was already reaching around her and inserting his credit card in the slot that had rejected hers with comparatively steady fingers, making Rayne catch her breath from his suffocating nearness and the achingly familiar scent of his cologne.

The girl with the sing-song voice looked up at him dreamily as she handed him the till receipt, with nothing having dared question his credit-worthiness!

'Have a good day, sir,' she said deferentially, beaming up at him and completely ignoring Rayne.

'You can't do this,' she protested as he tucked the till receipt with his credit card into the inside pocket of the dark suit jacket he was wearing. A hand-stitched, impeccably tailored suit worn with a white silk shirt that made her feel positively drab in comparison. Her beige cropped trousers with an elasticated waist and her one-size-too-big black T-shirt she'd bought to accommodate her tender and already expanding breasts just didn't compete.

'It seems I just did,' he remarked dryly. Already, with one arm, he was scooping up her tote bag, which was so full that she'd have had to carry it in both of hers, and with his other hand at her elbow, without any preamble, he said, 'Come on.'

'Where?' she demanded, flabbergasted.

Who did he think he was that he thought he could just march in here and start taking over her life? But as they were passing the counter in front of the in-store bakery, the sweet smell of the cakes was so cloying that a wave of nausea suddenly surged up inside her and had her fleeing towards the merciful sign she spotted just inside the Exit door.

When she emerged a little later, looking pale and with every trace of lipstick she had been wearing wiped clean away, King was waiting just a few steps from the door she had disappeared through.

A thick eyebrow climbed his forehead as Rayne approached. 'I thought you'd taken off through a back window or something,' he drawled, looking faintly amused. But then his eyes scanned her pinched wan face and those devastatingly handsome features took on a serious cast. 'You look dreadful,' he commented, his examining gaze too probing, too disconcertingly shrewd. 'Are you all right?'

No, I'm not! I'm having your baby! she wanted to fling at him bitterly, but knew that he wouldn't welcome hearing that.

'I thought about it,' she parried in response to his remark

about disappearing out of a window. 'But I thought I might get myself arrested, having already tried to use a pin number that wouldn't work.' It dawned on her now that she'd had so much on her mind she'd obviously inserted the wrong card.

'That isn't funny,' he chided softly.

'No, it isn't. It was downright embarrassing,' she expressed, feigning a tight little laugh. 'But I needn't have worried because you were on hand to compensate for my inadequacies.' With a sideways tilt of her head, she was unable to stop herself from adding, 'Just like old times, hmm?'

'And, just like old times, you're determined to keep me at arm's length and treat me like I'm your bitterest enemy.'

Well, what did he expect? Rayne thought poignantly. Instead, though, with the barest movement of her shoulder, she said, 'How's Mitch?'

'He's fine,' he said impatiently, as though he had no inclination to discuss his father just at that moment.

Rayne merely nodded, relieved at least that his father had recovered from his heart scare and she looked away from his indomitable son towards a stand of mixed doughnuts marked 'Tuesday's Best Buys', biting her lower lip.

'Why did you run away from me, Rayne?'

With her eyes downcast to hide the pain in them, she said flippantly, 'I needed the Ladies.'

His chest lifted on an impatient sigh. 'I didn't mean now. You know exactly what I'm talking about.'

'What did you expect me to do?' she queried accusingly. 'You thought I was a two-faced liar, to put it bluntly, and I couldn't convince you otherwise. Oh, I can understand why I hadn't exactly earned your undying trust, but I didn't deserve the things you said to me, so I thought it was best to leave.'

'Without telling me?' The disbelief he must have felt when he'd come back that day and realised that she'd gone was still apparent in his voice. 'By leaving me a polite little note?' She thought at first that it was pain pulling his features into tight, tense lines until, torturously, she reminded herself of how little he cared for her.

'OK.' She shrugged, trying to sound nonchalant rather than as if she were dying inside from her unrequited love for him. 'So I should have been grown-up and mature and told you I was leaving, and if the way I did it offended you then I apologise. I'm sorry. But you didn't exactly make me feel like sticking around.'

Yet that didn't stop her from wanting him now as fiercely and as desperately as she had ever done. Now, when he stood before her with that breath-catching vitality that paid homage to everything that was fit and strong and so intensely masculine, and which was making her weak with longing for his arms around her. Now, when she looked her worst and didn't have a chance in hell of ever securing his love. Now, when she was carrying his child…

She felt as if she would choke on her emotions—which, with the cloyingly sweet smell of confectionery that was wafting towards them, brought another wave of nausea rising up in her.

'Oh, heaven…' she breathed, bringing her hand to her mouth to try and curb the sickness, not wanting to make a fool of herself here in public. In front of him. Not wanting him to know…

'What the…?'

She steeled herself against his hard scrutiny, fighting her reaction to him, which wasn't helping her queasiness at all as strong masculine fingers caught her hand and brought it down from her face so that he could study her tense, wary features.

She looked pale. Too pale, he thought. In fact he would have said washed out, King decided, noticing the dark smudges under her eyes that made her appear fragile and exceedingly tired. And yet, even like that, she was still able to produce that familiar kick in his loins, he realised as his gaze slid over her body.

She was wearing an unflatteringly loose T-shirt over less than flattering trousers and beneath her top her beautifully full breasts seemed to be straining against the inadequate cups of her bra. Yet she was still the most beautiful woman he knew, with that long, sensuous red hair that was inviting him to run his fingers through it and those guarded green eyes that were half-veiled from him by her thick lashes as though she were concealing...

And suddenly it hit him with a force that for a few moments seemed to leave him winded.

'Are you pregnant?' he whispered huskily when he could speak again, his eyes narrowing into steel-blue speculative slits.

Rayne swallowed, grateful that the nausea was subsiding. 'What makes you think that?' she hedged.

'I wasn't born yesterday.'

It was no good denying it, she realised. He could calculate just as well as she could.

She tossed her head up, throwing caution to the winds. 'And what if I am?'

'If you are, then we've got rather a lot to talk about, don't you think?' he proposed, his half-veiled eyes inscrutable, his mouth grim.

'What is there to say?' She gave a hopeless little shrug. 'It wasn't supposed to happen.' Pray heaven he wouldn't think she would ask him for anything, she worried, mortified.

'But it clearly has. And, as the father...I take it I'm not being presumptuous in deducing that I *am* the father. All right,' he capitulated, putting up a hand to ward off the silent attack in her eyes. 'That wasn't intended as an insult.'

'*No?*' she uttered with biting accusation.

'No,' he underscored. 'And, as I was about to say...as your child's father, I think you'll agree that that gives me some rights as to how we proceed.'

'We?' Rayne emphasised, so bowled over by how he was

suddenly taking control that she was scarcely aware of being guided outside until they were in the car park.

The warmth of the late summer afternoon hit them after the cooling air-conditioning inside.

'Why didn't you tell me, Rayne?' he enquired, ignoring her last comment and aiming his remote control switch at the familiar black beast of the Lamborghini parked just a few strides away.

The vehicle's immediate response had heads turning to look, first at the car and then at the man who was rich enough to be driving it. Several pairs of feminine eyes feasted on him before sliding to Rayne, whom they quickly dismissed as too insignificant to be the lover of such a stupendously attractive man.

'It wasn't your fault,' she responded, unable to tell him that she had ached to hear from him again. That since finding out she was pregnant she had wanted to contact him but had balked at such a rash action, fearing what his reaction might be. He might think she had allowed herself to get pregnant to try and trap him, or just to get money out of him. After all, it wasn't as if they had even had a proper relationship…

'I hadn't realised in these circumstances that it was customary to apportion blame.'

She had told him she was on the Pill and he hadn't doubted her for a moment, even though she had been less than forthcoming with the truth about herself in the beginning. Still, his own behaviour towards her had been less than exemplary, when he had suspected her of just being after his father's money. Nor could he quite forgive himself for being so determined to get her into bed, even when he had felt that badly about her, even if his opinion of her had changed when he'd found out who she was and by the time they had eventually made love. The fact remained, though, that those abandoned few days had resulted in a child being conceived between them, and finding out as he'd just done had floored him.

'Aren't you angry?' Rayne enquired, watching his cool, economical movements as he opened the boot and placed her groceries inside.

'What's the point of being angry?' he stated with the descending boot lid punctuating his remark.

So he was, she thought, noticing a muscle pulling in his tight, tense jaw. And realising what he had just done, she said, 'I did bring my own car, you know. I can't leave it here.'

'We'll come back for it,' he told her, moving round the side of the car to open the passenger door. 'Because if you think I'm letting you get away from me again—and this time pregnant with my child—you can think again.' He gestured for her to get in.

'I was pregnant the first time,' she reminded him dryly, settling herself onto the luxuriously upholstered seat.

'Except that you didn't know. Otherwise, yes, I would have been exceedingly angry with you,' he assured her through the open door, slicing her flippant attempt to ease the awkward situation between them to pieces with the precision of a scythe.

'I suppose you think I engineered this as well, don't you?' she contested hopelessly when he slid onto the driver's seat beside her, guessing he would never ever accept her for the person she really was.

He could have, but he didn't, King thought, knowing her far better than she realised. He also knew that a woman of her calibre who had had enough gumption to do what she had for her father would never dream of stooping to such a thing, regardless of the insults he had flung at her that last morning in Monaco, which made him cringe now as he remembered them.

'I didn't come here to fight with you,' he stated, with one touch of his fingers bringing the powerful engine throbbing into life.

'Why did you come?' Rayne asked, trying not to think

about what those long skilled hands could do to her as she stared almost belligerently at the windscreen.

Seeing her chin raised in proud challenge against him, King wanted to take her in his arms and kiss her. But if he did, he knew she would probably only view his action as purely sexually motivated, and what he felt for this beautiful and complex woman was a lot more complicated than that.

'I wanted to see you,' he admitted heavily, restraining the impulse. 'We didn't exactly part on very amicable terms.'

'And whose fault was that?' Rayne looked directly into his dark brooding features now and, against all her powers of resistance, felt her heart lurch in her chest. 'You were horrible to me.'

'I was angry,' he told her truthfully, drawing his seat belt across his shoulder. 'That article had me doubting you. As it probably intended me to do,' he added with a self-effacing grimace. 'I know I overreacted and that I should have listened to you, but I never thought you'd leave—just like that.'

'Perhaps some people just don't like being treated as though they're the lowest of the low,' she said bitterly, wrenching her gaze from his dangerously handsome face and fastening her own seat belt with trembling hands, because just sitting here in such a confined space with him was making her so painfully aware of what they had shared.

'And for that I'm very sorry,' he expressed, wishing he'd swallowed his wounded masculine pride long before this instead of driving himself crazy with wanting to see her. 'It was wrong of me. That's why I came. To tell you to your face—and, in the circumstances, it's a good thing I did.'

He meant because of her pregnancy, because she couldn't imagine him being a man who would shirk his responsibilities.

'I don't want anything from you, if that's what you're imagining,' she put in quickly before he could say anything else.

'We'll see about that,' was all he said, reversing out of the space.

His features were set with purpose as the car roared away from the car park.

All he could think about was how his father—his family—had screwed up her family's life. And how they owed them big-time.

'Where are we going?' she asked, her forehead pleating.

'Just somewhere where we can talk.'

About the pregnancy. About how he could help support and maintain her and their baby, she decided from the way he was taking control. Unless, of course, he was simply intending to offer her the funds to ease the situation in what might possibly be—to him, at any rate—a far more convenient way, because he hadn't expected this outcome when he had come looking for her today.

'How did you know where to find me, anyway?' she asked tremulously when they were driving through the traffic, because the thought of him even entertaining that last scenario was making it almost painful to breathe. 'Did you just happen to be in that supermarket at the same time I was? Or do you have some sort of extra-terrestrial powers that homed in on me as soon as I stepped through the doors?' It occurred to her suddenly that she hadn't seen him buying anything for himself back there at the checkout.

'Neither,' he clarified. 'I called at your home and your mother told me where you were. I gather she wasn't too happy finding out from one of her neighbours on her return from Majorca that her daughter had been photographed with me in one of the tabloids.'

'No, she wasn't,' Rayne admitted, still cringing from the memory of both that article and her mother's response to it.

In fact, Cynthia Hardwicke had been horrified when Rayne had explained that she'd gone to Monaco to try and get the truth out of the Claybornes. 'Oh, Lorrayne!' the woman had expressed with an almost defeated slump to her shoulders. 'Why did you have to go and get involved?'

'And what did she say when you told her you were having my baby?' King asked, indicating to take a side road off the main highway.

Rayne drew in a deep breath. 'I haven't yet.'

The lifting of a masculine eyebrow expressed surprise and disbelief in equal measure. 'Don't you think it's time you did?'

'I'm going to,' Rayne returned with a niggling unease in her stomach. 'I just haven't wanted to give her anything else to worry about.'

'Anything else?' He sliced a glance her way. 'I take it she's all right? Health-wise?' he enquired succinctly.

Her forehead puckering, Rayne glanced quickly away from those far too perceptive eyes, saying in a rather unconvincing way, 'She's fine.'

She couldn't bring herself to tell him the truth. That Cynthia Hardwicke had developed further worrying complications. It was much too personal and painful to share with him at that moment. And anyway, there was the baby to talk about.

'I'm going to bring the baby up on my own, but I will allow you visiting rights, if that's what you want,' she managed to say quickly before her confidence failed her, and to let him know exactly what she was going to do. Let him know where he stood, in case he had any differing ideas as to what she should do about the precious little bundle of life she was carrying inside her. Because it was precious to her, regardless of the unfavourable circumstances in which it had been conceived.

'What do you mean?' he asked. 'If that's what I want?'

'I was only just saying—'

'No.'

'What do you mean? Don't you want visiting rights?' She couldn't believe he wouldn't want to see any child he might have created—even with her—and her eyes defied him to say anything that might indicate that he expected she might want to hurt her baby in any way.

'I think we should get married,' he said.

It was so far from what she had been expecting that she just sat there staring at him as he brought the car to a standstill in a quiet road beside the ancient iron gates of a local park.

'Because of the baby?' she croaked, hardly daring to hope that there might be some other motive driving him to suggest such a drastic step.

'Can you think of a better reason?' he suggested.

Only love, she supplied achingly, but she didn't say it, staring sightlessly through the open gates with their peeling blue paintwork at an enormous oak tree just inside the park, which looked as though it had stood like that, looking down on people, with their joys and sorrows, for centuries.

'I've known what it's like to go through childhood with only one parent,' he was reminding her now. 'And it wasn't a bowl of cherries, I can tell you. I don't want any child of mine having to go through what I did,' he stated grimly.

'It wouldn't. It would have two loving parents, even if—'

'With its time with them apportioned out, just how and when they thought fit?'

'We don't even know each other,' she reminded him, overwhelmed that he could decide such a thing after being acquainted with her for such a short time. Her legs felt weak and her heart was hammering like a drum-roll through her body.

'Couples wind up in the divorce courts after knowing each other for decades,' he commented dryly. 'I would have thought—for our child's sake, at least—you would be prepared to give us a chance.'

'And supposing we wound up hating each other? Or just not wanting each other…in that way any more?' Colour suffused her cheeks just from mentioning the passion that had gripped them both so profoundly while they had been in Monaco together.

'I don't think there will ever come a time when I won't want you—when *we* won't want each other—in that way, Rayne. The magnetic pull, or chemistry, or whatever you want to call this thing between us is far too strong. But, as for hating each other…well…if it doesn't work out within a few years we can always call it a day. But I want my child to be born legitimate, with two united parents and with my name.'

So that was all he was really concerned with. Legitimising his heir and protecting his rights and the rights of his child. Never mind about her. About how much she loved him! She didn't think she could enter into a marriage with him like that, knowing that if it didn't work out, if he wasn't happy, he would simply be prepared to 'call it a day'! Surely it would be better to walk away from him now, with her pride and her dignity intact, rather than at some later date when he realised that he couldn't love her, and when she was even more en-meshed in her feelings for him than she was now?

'I can't,' she heard herself uttering.

'How can you say that?' He was looking at her incredu-lously. 'Discount it just like that? I'm not only offering you a stable and comfortable home life for our child, but the best possible outcome in view of past…hostilities,' he supplied, finding the word he'd been searching for, 'between our fami-lies. Don't you see? This child we've created between us will not only have two loving parents to care for its welfare, but he'll also inherit the rewards of everything both our fathers—but particularly yours—created and missed out on. Doesn't he or she deserve that?'

Yes, Rayne thought, realising the poetic justice that lay in her marrying King and her children being the heirs to the Clayborne fortune—in combining their genes, their blood. In uniting their families.

But how could she, when she would only be tying herself

down to a man who was only marrying her because he'd made her pregnant? When he had come looking for her today, to do what, exactly? Express his regret for the way he had treated her—doubted her—and to take up where they had left off? Which was right back where they both wanted to be—in his bed! Instead of which, he now found himself faced with a child's future to plan, as well as having what he'd presumably hoped would be a willing mistress as his reluctant wife.

'I can't,' she murmured again. 'It wouldn't be right. We don't love each other, for a start.'

'Fair enough,' he agreed, not realising how deeply those two words had the power to hurt her. 'But we will have respect for each other—and loyalty, if we work at it—and perhaps this "love" that you're so wrapped up in will take care of itself.'

If only she could believe that! Rayne thought poignantly, but told him, 'You're not going to bully me into it.'

'And I wouldn't want to,' he expressed. 'All I'm asking is that, first and foremost, you consider the welfare of our child. And if that's not enough to persuade you into doing what's best for your baby, perhaps you'll be more inclined to come out from behind this idealised fantasy you're obviously harbouring about romantic love and think about how it could benefit your mother.'

'What do you mean?' she queried cagily, her tone both challenging and hurt.

He wasn't sure until then whether what he had garnered earlier when he had visited Cynthia Hardwicke's home was right. But now, from the pain that darkened those beautiful, yet guarded, eyes, and that same pain he'd seen on her face when he'd asked after her mother a few minutes ago, he wasn't left in any doubt.

'Your mother needs further treatment. Treatment, I suspect, that can only be paid for, and which neither of you can afford. How are you going to do it, Rayne? On the salary of a struggling freelance journalist? I can help you, if you'll let me. I can see to it that she receives all the necessary treatment and care she needs to help her optimize her chances of a good recovery.'

'Did she tell you that?' She sat looking out of the window, absently watching a squirrel foraging for food around the base of the oak tree and biting her lower lip to stem the emotion he knew she was battling against.

'Not in so many words,' he enlightened her. 'She said one or two things quite unintentionally that made me wonder and, seeing the way you were as soon as I spoke about her, it didn't take much to work it out.'

So what he was saying was that if she didn't marry him, not only would she be denying her child the best possible start in life, but also jeopardizing her mother's chances of a full recovery as well?

'And if you're thinking what I think you are,' he said, surprisingly astute, 'as things stand between us now, I doubt that she would even consider accepting any financial help from me, so I wouldn't insult her by trying to persuade her to. But, as her son-in-law, I think she'd be more inclined to accept what I was offering—particularly if the persuading came from her newly wedded and supposedly blissfully happy only daughter, with the means to give her mother everything she needed. I'd have to insist, though, that we get married with no time to lose, since it's imperative that she's taken care of as quickly as possible.'

So, in short, if anything happened to her mother when she could have had the chance to prevent it, she'd have it on her conscience for the rest of her life.

'Put like that, I don't really have much choice, do I?' she murmured, resigning herself to her fate of becoming King Clayborne's wife. It was something she had once longed for and yet now, when faced with the reality of it happening, she was just left feeling numb and chilled by an aching regret. 'As you say, there's far more to consider in all this than simply what either of us really wants, isn't there?' she uttered with a false show of bravado.

'Yes, there is.' His own regret was clear from the way his breath shivered through him. He was simply doing the right thing. Nothing more. 'But not as I say, Rayne. As circumstances beyond our own desires, thoughts and feelings dictate.'

So he would be legitimising the Clayborne heir and seeing that all the treatment her mother needed from now on would be taken care of, which was a relief and a mercy, Rayne realised, beyond her wildest hopes. But King Clayborne was a high-flyer and used to associating with beautiful and celebrated women. Supposing he got bored with her and chose to end the marriage at some later date? What then?

Then he would have secured his rights to his child and ensured that he would always be a part of that child's life, but what about her? Could she bear the pain of losing him when it felt as if her very reason for having been born was simply to love him? She had to, because he was offering her mother the chance she needed, and she knew that any amount of personal unhappiness that might follow would be worth it to see her mother well again. There was no question of that.

She only knew that while she and King were man and wife she would give it everything she had to make their marriage work—to try and make him love her. After all, if she could, she thought, and they had a lovely baby to focus on as well, would there ever be any reason for him to go?

CHAPTER ELEVEN

THE register office wedding had been booked for two weeks ahead, and it was to be a small private affair with just a handful of guests attending.

King had already been having discussions with a top consultant about Cynthia Hardwicke's condition. Just as he had predicted, at first she had been strongly opposed to accepting any financial help.

But, after being told that she was going to be a grandmother—something she admitted to having guessed, despite Rayne's secrecy about it—and then being told that King—whom she had also guessed was the father of her future grandchild—actually intended to marry her daughter, it wasn't long before she finally gave in. Wooed, Rayne suspected, not only by the prospect of the coming baby, but also by King's inimitable charm.

In the meantime, regarding her only daughter's wedding, Cynthia Hardwicke was determined to offer all the maternal help and support she could.

'You don't mind, do you?' Rayne asked her a couple of days later, when they were browsing together around the bridal department of the exclusive London store.

'About you marrying a Clayborne?' Her mother's mouth tugged speculatively. 'I want whatever you want for yourself, Lorrayne. I just wish you'd told me you were having his baby. Told me you were pregnant without my having to guess.'

'I just didn't want to say anything to upset you,' Rayne told her ruefully. 'You aren't too disappointed in me, are you?'

'I could never be disappointed in you, darling. Just as long as you're happy,' her mother emphasised.

'I love him, if that's what you mean.'

'And does he love you?'

Rayne glanced away.

'I see.' Her mother's softly spoken statement held a wealth of understanding. 'Oh, darling...'

'But he will,' Rayne told her nonchalantly, feigning an interest in the billowing ivory satin yards of one of the extortionately priced wedding dresses she was fingering on the rail. 'I've got enough love for both of us,' she tagged on as determinedly as she could. 'And the welfare of his baby means everything to him. We can't fail to make it work,' she stressed, trying to convince her mother, even if she couldn't quite convince herself. And suddenly, from nowhere, the question sprang into her mind so that, before she knew it, she was asking, 'Mum...were you always happy with Dad?'

Cynthia Hardwicke's interest in the fabric her daughter was holding seemed to be as distracted, Rayne thought, as her own. 'We had our ups and downs.'

'But wasn't there ever a time when...when you thought it just wasn't going to work out?' She deliberately kept her attention on the dress but out of the corner of her eye saw the way Cynthia Hardwicke's forehead creased.

'Why all these questions?' Her mother sounded, Rayne thought, just like she did when she used to pat her on the head and tell her brightly that everything was going to be all right when she didn't really know if it would be. 'Are you really so unsure of King?'

'No.' Because how could she doubt the package that he'd laid out for her in black and white? She knew exactly how he felt—and where she stood. 'I just wanted to be certain that you're all right with what I'm doing because...' she couldn't look at her mother at all now as she said '…because you and Dad were so happy. And because you thought, like I did, that King had supported Mitch in stealing Dad's ideas from him and—'

'Which is why you went over to see Mitch Clayborne when I was away. Which is why, had I known, I'd have stopped you getting involved in what happened. For a start, Lorrayne, I've never held anything against King.'

'You haven't?' Now it was Rayne's turn to frown.

'Your father signed something which, on paper, gave us no legal right to pursue any claim for that software. Mitch and your father had agreed to launch it in their joint names but there were reasons why King's father didn't honour his promise. I don't know if I should be telling you this or any good way to say it, but Mitchell's wife and your father…'

As Cynthia hesitated, Rayne looked at her quickly now, clarity dawning in her wide, shocked eyes.

'You *knew* about that?' she said.

'Yes, darling, I did. And I gather that you now know about it too.'

'Oh, Mum!' Emotion welled into Rayne's eyes as she hugged her mother, regardless of who might be watching, not that there were more than one or two other customers browsing around the spectacularly designed gowns. 'Why didn't you tell me?'

'I didn't want to hurt you, darling. Or do anything to destroy the picture you had of your father. I know how much you loved him—and how much he loved you. And apart from that one foolish indiscretion, he was a good man.'

'You should have told me,' Rayne remonstrated softly, releasing her, wishing her mother hadn't had to bear the brunt of her heartache alone.

'Just as you should have told me when you first suspected you were pregnant,' Cynthia scolded gently, tenderly cupping Rayne's cheek. 'I suppose that makes us both a pair of stubborn, independent women—and both far stronger than each of us have given the other credit for being.'

'I'm sorry,' Rayne breathed, comforted by that maternal strength that made her realise just how precious her mother was to her. 'I thought you were totally blinded by love and would have cracked up if you'd ever found out what Dad had done. Oh, Mum! Why did you stay?'

'I stayed because he needed me—and to hold our home together,' Cynthia told her philosophically. 'Without that, our little family, which meant everything to me, would simply have fallen apart.'

And she'd thought her mother was the shrinking violet of her two parents! The one who had needed all the help and support and protection from any emotional stress when, in fact, it had been the other way around.

She only hoped that she would have the same kind of strength to support her husband and her child or children whenever they needed her as her mother had done throughout those difficult years, and she thanked her lucky stars that Cynthia Hardwicke would be given the chance to enjoy having grandchildren.

And that surely had to compensate for the fact that had she not gone to Monaco—which she wouldn't have done, Rayne decided painfully, had she known the truth—she wouldn't now be suffering agonies of doubt about marrying the man she loved, a man who was only marrying her because she was carrying his child.

It was proposed that after they were married they would live in King's country home, which was within commuting distance of London. The house took Rayne's breath away the day King first took her there.

An exclusively designed and totally modern building constructed mainly of glass, the faultless architecture of its various storeys seemed to grow out of the hillside, rising up with the trees that gave it its privacy and seclusion. The garden wrapped itself around the house, a garden filled with nooks and secret pathways, which would be a dream, Rayne decided, for children to explore, while a terrace at the back gave onto manicured lawns which tumbled down to the River Thames and a private mooring where King kept his boat.

'How the other half live,' she remarked dryly, with a grimace, because she couldn't imagine herself ever living in such a stupendous place, let alone as King Clayborne's wife.

'No. How *we're* going to live,' he corrected her, with his arm going around her as he guided her to the front door. 'You're going to be my other half, Rayne. We're going to be a unit. A family.'

'Based on accidental pregnancy and physical attraction?' she reminded him pointedly, with her head cocked at an angle.

'Based on two people pulling together to do what's best.'

And that was that, she realised with a little shiver of longing, wishing she could have taken more pleasure in the luxury of her surroundings. The type of pleasure any bride-to-be who loved with the knowledge of how much her future husband loved her would have taken in being told that this was going to be her future home, she thought. But even so, she still couldn't help being bowled over by the immediate impact of wealth combined with exquisite taste as he let her into the house.

This place had it all, from the touches of ebony and Italian marble to the exclusive antiques, body-sinking sofas and the Chinese silks that hung from the endless windows, which allowed one to feel part of the great outdoors while maximising the use of light. There was even a white baby grand piano standing in its own acres of floor space, enhanced by a couple of the many large and luxuriant plants that were growing about the place, obviously thriving because of all the light.

'I didn't know you played!' she exclaimed gleefully, mov-

ing over to the piano, considering then how little she did
know about him.

'I don't.'

The lid was open, exposing the keys, and she'd started running her fingers lightly over them. But, realising what he'd
just said, she looked up at him quickly, her gaze questioning
as he came and stood beside her.

'Then why…'

But it had already dawned and her heart skipped a beat
when she saw the almost amused twist to his lips.

She remembered telling him that day on the yacht that
she'd learned to play the piano as a child, and that her parents had sold theirs when she'd lost interest. She hadn't told
him that it had been sold to help pay off their debts, but she
had said that she intended to take up the instrument again as
soon as she could. One day. One day when she had saved up
enough money to afford one that wasn't too expensive, but
she hadn't told him that either. And now…

'I can't believe you've done this,' she breathed, standing
there with tears in her eyes.

'Then believe this.'

Suddenly his arm was around her waist and he was pulling her against him.

Every nerve leaped in answering response.

As always, when they started to kiss, it was never enough
and hungrily, drowning in the scent and touch and feel of each
other, they started ripping one another's clothes off, Rayne's
chequered tie-blouse and jeans, King's jacket and shirt and tie
strewn over the floor leading from the opulent sitting room
to the foot of the huge round bed two storeys up, where they
made love as if it was the first time for each of them.

Afterwards, lying there in the crook of King's arm
amongst navy-blue satin sheets and cushions and watching
the sun dappling the trees which seemed as much a part of
the magnificent bedroom as its coved ceiling and windows,

Rayne thought of all King was offering her besides marriage. Security for her child. Help for her mother. He had even put in a bid for a beautifully restored cottage nearby so that she wouldn't have to worry about being too far from her mother. And on top of everything else—the piano.

Even if he could never give her his love, Rayne mused, silently anxious, it was obvious he would be generous with everything else. And whatever else was lacking in their marriage, she wasn't in any doubt that he wanted her physically at least. She only hoped that she could be content to let that be enough.

King flew up to Edinburgh the next day for a couple of days, while Rayne carried on with plans for the forthcoming wedding.

She put a deposit on a gown—something simple with a lacy bodice and an A-line skirt that needed a bit of adjustment on the waist to take account of her pregnancy—and which she had arranged to collect at the beginning of the next week. Then she spent a couple of hours wandering around shelves of cuddly toys and wallowing in aisles of miniature jumpers and dresses and smart little dungarees, wishing that, while she was looking forward to this coming baby with so much love and expectation, the thought of her imminent wedding wasn't churning her up so much inside.

The following morning brought a letter from Mitch, back in his own home in the Loire, full of regret that she had left Monaco in the way she had before he had returned from the clinic and—in a rather roundabout way—for what had happened in the past between him and her father. The letter then went on to express his surprise at hearing that she would be tying the knot with, as he put it, *his only son*, although he sounded thrilled that King would be giving him an heir, and equally thrilled that it was going to be with her.

His letter continued on a rather self-congratulatory note.

*I told you you'd be a good match for him and that he
needed someone like you to stand up to him once in a
while, didn't I? And now you have, and I can't think of
anyone I'd rather have as the mother of my grandchild,
or as my daughter-in-law, little Lorri.*

That last bit was gratifying but, contrarily, it lowered her
spirits a little too.

The way he had addressed her reminded her of being
young and optimistic about love and romance and life in
general, and of those days she'd spent in her father's office,
hungry for any chance meeting with King. She'd ached for
him then, but not as she ached for him now—with a woman's
passion. It was a lonely, desolate aching for him now, even
though she was carrying his child, because she knew that he
wasn't marrying her for the right reasons. Such as love and
mutual trust and respect. Such as the fact that he couldn't
live without her. How could he be, when they had known
each other for such a short space of time? No, he probably
felt guilty and as though he owed her something for what his
family had done to hers, and so he couldn't just abandon her
with his child on top of that.

With that less than flattering thought, she took the train out
to her future home, walking from the village because the day
was so beautifully warm and mellow, although she felt all-
in by the time she had let herself into the magnificent house.

King was still away on business in Edinburgh and, as
Cynthia Hardwicke was feeling well enough to accompany
her friend to see a West End show and had decided to spend
the night in town, Rayne felt it was a good opportunity to do
some measuring up in what she had chosen to be their baby's
room, and then stay at the house until King returned the following afternoon.

He had given her carte blanche to do whatever she wanted
in terms of redecorating or refurnishing the house, but when

she'd taken a leisurely appraisal of his home she realised with surprise that his taste suited her perfectly.

It was dark by the time she finished her measuring up.

Pleased at finding that the little pieces of white furniture she'd picked out for the nursery would fit the spaces she had designated for them perfectly, she decided, as she was feeling extraordinarily tired tonight, to run herself a warm bath in the luxuriously appointed master bathroom at the top of the house, then take herself off to bed.

Its gargantuan proportions and its abundance of dark scattered satin cushions and pillows made the bed look sensuously inviting.

Too inviting, Rayne decided when the memory of making love there with King and the thought of how many times he would make love to her again between those billowing sheets had her aching for him with a need that darkened her eyes and put a pink tinge across her cheeks.

Having soaked in a long, luxurious bath, she stepped out and wound a huge white fluffy towel around herself.

She felt heavy and aching, and wished that King was there. And suddenly, glancing absently at the towel with which she had been drying herself, she froze, shock ripping through her with the trembling realisation of what was happening.

CHAPTER TWELVE

'You have to tell King,' Cynthia Hardwicke advised, already in a taxi on her way over. 'If you're losing the baby he has a right to know—and now!'

'I can't. Not yet,' Rayne told her, fighting back tears.

How could she tell her mother that she couldn't bear to drag him back from Edinburgh? That, on top of all her fear and misery about starting a miscarriage, she wouldn't be able to bear hearing him saying all the things he thought he should say to her when she guessed that, deep down, he would probably be nursing a huge sense of relief?

Because what man would be crazy enough to tie himself down to a woman he didn't love—and after so short an acquaintance? Particularly a man in King's position, unless he felt he had to—which he clearly did.

She hadn't even wanted to tell her mother, not only because she hated having to worry her. But also because, ridiculously, she'd felt that until she did tell someone, it might not be happening.

But it was, and so finally she had rung her friend Joanne in France because she had felt so frightened.

'You must tell your mother,' her friend had urged when she'd found out King was away. 'You can't stay there on your own.'

So she had, and shortly afterwards Cynthia Hardwicke

arrived, not long after the doctor who Rayne had called to ask for advice.

'If there's no pain and you're not haemorrhaging, then I won't rush you off to hospital,' the out-of-hours locum told Rayne briskly. 'At this early stage of a pregnancy there will be nothing anyone can do to prevent a miscarriage happening once it's already started,' the woman informed her a little more sympathetically. 'But if there are any problems—' she reeled off a few '—don't hesitate to call A & E.'

So that was that, Rayne thought numbly, hearing the woman's car pulling away, thinking about what she'd advised if things got any worse.

Later, with her mother having taken herself off to bed in one of the guest rooms at Rayne's insistence, she tried to get some sleep, but her thoughts wouldn't let her. Because what could be worse than losing the baby she already had so much feeling for? Unless it was to be told what she already knew deep down inside—that she was going to lose King as well?

Unable to rest, she got up and, slipping on the long ivory silk robe she had brought with her over her short matching nightdress, she stole quietly downstairs to the kitchen.

The fridge was well-stocked by the woman King employed to come in twice a week to clean and, pouring herself some juice, Rayne moved into the sitting room, where a full harvest moon was throwing a shaft of amazingly bright light over the white and ebony keys of the piano.

After losing her father—and then with her mother being ill—life had suddenly become so precious to her. And now...

She dropped down onto the piano stool, her fingers tense around her glass. She had desperately wanted this baby, she thought achingly. After getting over the initial shock of finding out that she was pregnant, she had welcomed the baby as part of them, but especially as part of King—a man she had been in love with since she was eighteen. But he wouldn't have wanted her as his wife if he hadn't unintentionally—and probably very regrettably, she decided with an acute ache in her chest—made her pregnant in the first place. She'd welcomed it as a symbol of her newly rekindled love for him—the love she knew she would always feel for him—even if that love was never reciprocated—and she had wondered over and over again during the past two and a half months when exactly it was she had conceived.

Was it that night he had come back to the house looking so devilishly dishevelled and yet devastated, too? The night when her intuition alone had told her that he was every bit the man she had always hoped he was? Or the next day on his yacht, when she had glimpsed the loneliness in him and when, rediscovering her love she had ached to fill the void she had sensed deep down inside him?

The day he had surprised her by playing her favourite music...

Setting her glass aside, with one finger she absently picked out the first few bars of the poignant theme until, tortured beyond belief, she threw the piano lid closed and collapsed, sobbing, over it, pouring out her grief with the pain of her loss and the agony of even more loss to come.

Why would he still want to marry her when he discovered that she was having a miscarriage? What was there to keep him with her when there was no other reason for him to stay?

She must have fallen asleep like that—a pale figure slumped over the piano with her head resting on her arms—because that was how King found her an hour or so later when he came quickly and silently across the room.

She hadn't been upstairs when he'd come in, making straight for the bedroom, having driven back from Edinburgh like a madman, though the bedclothes were rumpled and the lamp on the cabinet on her side of the bed was on, as though she'd only just got up.

'Rayne?' He wanted to reach out and touch the pale slope of her shoulder but was afraid that if he did he would startle her, and he wanted to avoid that. 'Rayne,' he repeated in a tone that was soft and deep.

She made a soft sound like a whimper as she lifted her head, and anxiously he wondered if she was in pain.

'You're home,' she murmured weakly, with a surge of relief and then sadness washing over her as everything came back to her. She couldn't believe he was standing there right beside the piano. She'd thought he was coming back tomorrow.

'Cynthia rang me.' The moonlight had shifted since she'd first come in here, slashing across the wooden floor behind him so that his face was in shadow. 'Why didn't you?'

So her mother had telephoned him after all! He sounded so pained that she looked up at him questioningly as she angled herself around towards him on the stool, absently remembering that she'd given Cynthia his cellphone number in case her mother couldn't reach her at any time.

'I couldn't,' she sighed, unable to tell him the reason why. 'I didn't want you dashing home.' As he evidently had. 'I thought it would be best to wait until the morning to tell you.'

'That you were losing our baby?'

There was incredulity in his voice. But the way he bracketed the two of them together brought emotion welling up in her again, and it took every ounce of willpower she possessed to restrain it.

'Shouldn't you be in bed?' As he laid a gentle hand on her shoulder he heard her catch her breath as though she didn't welcome the contact and was recoiling from it, although she gave no physical indication of doing so. 'You're cold,' he observed, horrified, touching his hand to her cheek. He couldn't believe how cold. 'Here.'

Rayne heard rather than saw him shrugging out of his jacket.

She sucked in a breath as the warmth of it came around her back and shoulders. His body warmth, she thought achingly, drowning in the familiar scent of him that clung to it, sitting there like a limp doll while he pulled it around her as though she were a small child.

He dropped to his haunches in front of her.

'Are you sure?' he whispered, holding on to her, his eyes almost level with hers.

He meant about the baby and she nodded. 'The doctor seemed to think so and I…I don't feel pregnant any more.'

She heard him draw in a breath and saw, in the dim light, his lashes come down as he nodded his head. Accepting it, she thought. Before she could. Without any problem.

Even so, as his arms came around her, offering her the comfort she guessed he thought she would need, she couldn't stop herself from straining towards him, clinging to him, breathing in the scent of him first-hand this time, and wondering how many more times he would hold her like this before he finally released her from their commitment.

'You know what this means, don't you?' she said, making herself deal with it—say it—before he could. 'It means we don't have to get married any more.'

Whatever it was King had been expecting, it wasn't that, and coming as it did so soon after being told that the child he had anticipated wasn't going to be, felt like a double slap in the face. Like the one she'd given him when they were in Monaco, only harder and more incisively targeted. He wondered how much duress she must have felt under to have agreed to marry him in the first place.

'We'll talk about that later,' he said thickly, getting to his feet, 'but first of all I think we should get you back to bed.'

She didn't protest as he lifted her up as effortlessly as if she were the child she had envisioned herself as a few moments ago. She wanted these last moments with him. To memorize how it felt to have her arms around his neck, his warmth, his latent strength, to be this close to him when there would be so many cold and lonely days to follow that would find her forever wondering what might have been, and what being King's wife and the mother of his children would have been like.

Perhaps it couldn't cling on because it knew you didn't love me, she thought, torturing herself, and drew no consolation from the knowledge that pregnancies of women who were happily settled with their partners could often end in miscarriage. Especially with a first pregnancy, the doctor had said when she had been trying to reassure her, but she hadn't been listening, concerned only with what was happening to *her* baby, the little life she had been nurturing inside her.

King bore her up the four flights of stairs without bothering to switch on the lights. The moon shining in the long and wide windows on each landing put a silvery wash over the stairs, throwing their shadows onto the side wall that ran up from the lowest storey.

They looked like tragic lovers, he thought with unrestrained cynicism, aware of the straining bulk that was his own body and the slender arms wrapped around him, of the way the feminine head was angled so that it looked to be almost touching his.

He was mourning this child, he realised in that moment, and found himself acknowledging that he *had* wanted it—and more than he could ever have imagined possible. He had wanted the responsibility of another human being to care for. Part of himself. Someone he could always be there for in the way that neither of his own parents had ever been there for him. It had felt like a chance to redress the balance. A chance to put things right. And it had seemed like a good enough reason for accepting its existence when he'd given Rayne little option about marrying him and had hustled her through the arrangements for the wedding day after day.

But was it? he asked himself as he carried her into the softly lit, splendid opulence of the master bedroom. Because how much thought had he given to what she might want? And what was right for her? And now he answered himself truthfully. Very little.

But now, as he set her on her feet and she turned to let his jacket slip off her shoulders onto the bed, he saw from the lamplight, and for the first time, how shockingly desolate she looked. Her face, cleansed of make-up, looked pale and gaunt, and he could see that her eyes were red-rimmed and puffy with crying.

And suddenly it dawned on him how much she must have wanted this baby. Wanted it—even though she hadn't wanted him.

'Oh, my poor love…' His arm was still round her middle and now he caught her to him, not caring how weak it might make him seem or how he sounded as he buried his lips in her hair and, in a voice that seemed wrenched from him, he uttered, 'I'm sorry. I'm really so very, very sorry.'

For what? Rayne wondered wretchedly, aching to clasp him to her but only allowing her hands to rest lightly on the straining contours of his muscled back. For making her love him in the first place? For making her pregnant and having to watch her lose the most precious gift he could ever have given her? Or for not being able to love her and for leaving her just as soon as he considered it felt right for him to do so?

'Don't,' she demurred, and wished it had come out sounding less like a plea when he didn't let her go, but urged her gently down to sit on the bed beside him.

Just as gently, then, he put an arm under her knees and lifted her legs onto the mattress so that she could relax against the mountain of cushions that were still stacked up on his side of the bed.

'It meant everything to you, this baby. Didn't it?' he said with a surge of hope that was quickly quashed when she looked down and away from him with her lips pressed almost mutinously tight.

'What did you imagine?' she invited him to tell her, and

with such a wobble in her voice that he realised it was threatening emotion that was making her look like that.

She didn't look at him, but kept staring at some point between the door and the mirrored wall of endless wardrobes, waiting for him to tell her that she was young and strong. That one day she'd have more babies, and with someone she really wanted to be with, but he didn't. He just kept looking at her with that fathomless emotion etching his face, understanding at least that that wasn't what she needed to hear right now.

Unless, of course, he'd guessed that she'd only ever wanted his, and that this baby was so special to her because of all they had already shared and because of how hopelessly she loved him. In which case, was that emotion she would have so dearly liked to believe was shared anguish in him really only generated by sympathy for her?

'You're going to have to cancel the wedding,' she advised him, choked, because if pity was all he felt for her then she couldn't bear it.

He didn't look at her as his breath shuddered through his lungs. 'We'll talk about it tomorrow,' he said, starting to get up.

Rayne shot out a hand to stop him and, feeling the bunching muscles of his arm, quickly retracted it, reminded too poignantly of how exquisite he was and of just how much pleasure they had known together.

'No, now,' she stressed, steeling herself against the emotional pain.

'All right, then.' His shoulders seemed to slump from the heavy breath he exhaled, a resigned posture that matched the note of resignation in his voice. 'Fire away.'

'We're going to have to lose some deposits. And I know this hasn't exactly gone the way you planned...' She dragged in a breath, finding it took every ounce of her mental strength to put on a brave face. 'I can bear some of the expense myself, but I can't yet pay you back for what you've already arranged for Mum. But if you let her treatment go ahead, I'll slave…I'll slave day and night to save up and—'

'Enough!' His fist came down on his knee, punctuating his barely rasped command and, through her misery, Rayne was amazed to realise that he was trembling. His voice was trembling too and his eyes were darkened by an emotion she could almost touch. 'What sort of hard, insensitive individual do you think I am?'

He had asked her something like that before. Ten weeks ago. When they were in Monaco. But she couldn't think about that right now, only why the groan that seemed to come from deep in his chest sounded like that of an animal in pain.

'Have you ever considered for one moment that I might be just as cut up over losing this baby as you are? Why can a woman only feel pain? Loss? Regret? And had it even occurred to you that I might not want to cancel the wedding?'

'What?' Through the mire of her unhappiness, his question awakened a spark of something in her not unlike hope.

'Yes,' he affirmed on a laboured breath. 'Crazy though that might seem to you, I still want to go ahead and do everything we were planning.'

'Why?' Rayne enquired, stupefied. Then, as it suddenly dawned on her, 'Because you feel sorry for me?' she remembered, hurting. 'Because you think you owe it to me?'

His body had been half-turned away from her, but now he shifted his position so that he was facing her full on and she could see the pained incredulity in his eyes.

'Hadn't it occurred to you either that I might…just might…' it was a soft reprimand '…be in love with you?' he rasped.

Now it was her turn to look incredulous, and yet there was warmth starting to trickle through the cold emptiness she had been feeling inside.

'But…how can you be?' she challenged breathlessly. Her head felt cloudy and yet her heart was racing. 'I mean…we haven't…'

'Haven't known each other long enough?' he supplied. The ghost of a smile was trying to play around one side of his mouth now. 'You already admitted to being mad about me before. And if your response to me whenever I touch you is anything to go by, I'd say you still are,' he took the chance on saying. After all, he thought, what was there to lose? 'All right,' he went on, bolder now that he could see incredulity being dissipated by the warmth that lit her eyes. 'You might think I'm crazy. And perhaps I am,' he said with a self-mocking pull of his lips. 'But I've never been in love before so I can't judge what this feeling is. But if love is never wanting to let you go, that it would devastate me if I were to lose you, and wanting you—and only you—to be the mother of my children, then I'm in love.'

'Oh, King...'

She sat forward and grasped his arm, laying her head against the strong, hard support of his shoulder. There were tears in her eyes as his arms came round her now, but they were shining with love and warmth and the knowledge that while she was losing something so precious, she could bear it if he was beside her, loving her. Sharing, not just the good times, but times like now, when she needed him. So much...

'There's no one who's ever made me feel like you do,' he murmured huskily into the perfumed silk of her hair, holding her as though he would never let her go.

'You mean drive you to distraction,' she suggested, sniffing back emotion, feeling suddenly that there was so much to hold on to, even if right now there was such a dark cloud hanging over her—over them both.

'Like I want to take care of you,' he scolded softly, proving it to her as he set her tenderly back against the pillows just in case it might be harming her to give into this need to hold her and keep her sitting there, locked in his arms. 'Like I want to grow with you. Learn with you and from you—because we both have so much to learn from and about each other, dearest. Comfort you—as you so badly need that from me now…' His voice was thickened by emotion and when he placed his hand lightly over her abdomen she could so easily have wept. But she didn't, for his sake as well as her own, battling against her hormones and a whole flood of feeling for this wonderful man as he murmured, 'Would you let me do that for you, Rayne?'

'Oh, King,' she expressed again. 'If you only knew how much I want that. Have wanted it. And not like the lovesick teenager you called me and that I know I was, but as I am—as we are—now. I feel I've known you all my life. Even when you thought I was too young for you and you weren't even aware of me.'

'Oh, I was aware of you,' he confessed, smiling down at her from where he lounged, his head resting on his bent arm, his long length stretched out on the bed beside her now. 'Or at least of your presence. And very much so,' he admitted, trailing an index finger down the soft curve of her cheek. 'From the first time I saw you, until the last. While you were there in the office for that short time I couldn't stop looking at you— or at least the outline of you—through that frosted glass, and I had to keep pulling myself up short and reminding myself that I shouldn't. You were a crazy kid and I was just starting out. And, to test my resistance even further, when you weren't there your father never stopped talking about you,' he remembered wryly.

Her eyes darkened a little as he mentioned her father. 'Talking about me?' she asked, curious. 'In what way?'

'Like how, after slipping a disc and losing the use of its legs, you sacrificed a trip to the States with your friends to look after the family dog. Which meant carrying him everywhere,' he outlined, sounding impressed, 'until he could walk again.'

'Well, he recovered,' she stated assertively, remembering now that rare moment in the office when King had singled her out to enquire about the spaniel; remembered how she'd hugged that moment to her for weeks.

'But only thanks to you,' he reminded her. 'The same girl who wanted to support every children's and animal charity that posted a flyer through her door, while training to run a half marathon for Oxfam. The girl who looked like a cross between the scarecrow in the Wizard of Oz and the Bride of Dracula. The girl who was crazy about Dvořák's music...'

A flush touched her cheeks from the pleasure of knowing how King had retained so much about her. It surprised her, too, to learn about all her father had said.

'No matter where he was planning to go, or how much he might have thought he wanted my stepmother, he never stopped loving you, Rayne,' King told her, cannily sensing everything that she was feeling. 'And I don't think *I* have—subconsciously,' he admitted candidly—amazingly—to her, 'because it was one hell of a testimonial to deal with for a young man who was trying to stay immune. I was planning to ask you out—given a year or two. When you'd grown up a bit and I didn't have so much on my mind. But within weeks your father and Mitch had that blow up. And then, after that night when I called round to your house to see Grant and you flew at me like I was some sort of demon, I knew I'd blown whatever chances I'd had of getting to know you better.'

What he was saying amazed her and, looking up at him now, she wondered how any man could be so handsome, as well as having such inner strength and tenderness, as she allowed her fingers to revel in the texture of his dark, un-shaven jaw.

'I know I came over all possessive and overbearing about... the baby,' he went on with some hesitancy, 'but ultimately I knew it was the only chance I had of keeping you with me—in my life,' he disclosed hoarsely, making her tremble with the depth of her feeling for him as his thumb moved lovingly over the soft outline of her mouth. 'Can you ever forgive me?' he asked.

'Only if you'll promise to always stay as determined to keep me with you,' she murmured, feeling as if her heart were overflowing. 'I couldn't bear it if I lost you.' And realising that she hadn't actually told him in as many words, she whispered from the depths of her soul, 'I love you, King.'

'I promise,' he whispered back, bending to kiss her, oh, so softly on her mouth. 'And now, my love, I think it's time you got some rest.'

The wedding was going ahead as planned for the end of the following week but, sitting there in the waiting area of the pregnancy unit while Rayne had gone for her ultrasound scan, King wished fervently that she wasn't having to go through all this beforehand. Seeing doctors. The check-ups. Having to be prodded and poked about. All quite routine and happily anticipated when it was to assess how your little one was developing, but not under these circumstances. Agitatedly, he tossed down the magazine he had been thumbing through without having read a word. Not like this.

He had wanted to be with her but she had insisted that he wait outside and, very reluctantly, he had complied with her wishes. He guessed she didn't want him to see how upset it made her to be told categorically that her pregnancy was over.

She'd need a lot of care and consideration over the weeks ahead, he realised, hiding his own regret and disappointment behind his usual practised calm as he promised himself he would do everything it took to make this difficult time easier for her.

She was crying when she came out of the room beyond.

She'd promised him she would be brave, but he could see at once that the ordeal had proved too much for her, even if she was doing her best to hide it from the other happily expectant couple who had been sitting opposite him.

'I should have been there with you,' he said, berating himself as he reached her side and put a consoling arm around her shoulders. 'I shouldn't have listened to you. I should have come in.'

He took her hand in his—the one with the emerald and diamond engagement ring he had brought back from Edinburgh and placed on her finger this morning—a token of his love, a sign that he was marrying her for who she was: the woman he was crazy about—and understood how, right then, she was too over-wrought to speak.

It wasn't until they were outside in the mellow sunshine that she finally gave rein to her emotion, sobbing against his shoulder while he held her close and felt each convulsive sob like a pain in his heart.

At last she managed to get a grip on herself and, as she looked up at him now, he could see that she was trying to shrug off her outpouring of emotion, to even smile at him through the mist of her tears.

'Our baby...' She was trembling; choking on the words. 'They found a heartbeat. It was visible on the ultrasound! They said it was good and strong and it's got the right number of beats per minute! I'm still pregnant, King! That doctor was wrong.'

If she could have described the effect those words had on his face then she would have said it was like coming out into brilliant sunshine after being in a long, dark tunnel. But then she still couldn't quite believe herself that they had both been handed back such a beautiful miracle. 'They said it *could* have been a threatened miscarriage but, if it wasn't, then what happened isn't entirely uncommon. It could have been caused by possible hormone fluctuation, which is why I stopped feeling pregnant. And they said that that's not uncommon either, particularly at this stage of our pregnancy.'

King could scarcely believe what she was saying. He was

still going to be a father! He felt like jumping up with a terrific *Whoop!* and reaching for the sky.

It also touched him immensely how she had said 'our' pregnancy. It meant that she was going to share every part and every minute of his child's development with him over the coming months. Meant that this wonderful woman, who had started out as just a flitting figure he wanted to deny being attracted to, was having his baby, and was never going to shut him out of her life—or be separated from him—again. Meant that whatever problems lay ahead, they could deal with them. Together. Her mother's health. Mitch. And any other trials and tribulations that came their way.

'I love you,' he told her, placing a hand on the yet gentle swell of her middle. 'Both of you,' he murmured, and the depth of his unmistakable love produced an answering emotion in Rayne.

When she responded, standing on tiptoe to kiss him, her face was glowing, King noticed, her eyes moist and sparkling, but sparkling now, he acknowledged, with tears of joy.

'Do you realise the papers are going to have a field day when they realise that, not only are we married, but that we've already started a family?' she breathed, slightly in awe of all the attention that the news would attract initially.

'Let them!' King invited, smiling broadly, locking her to his side as they moved leisurely back to the car, and from the pride and happiness she could see and feel emanating from him at the prospect of being a husband and father, Rayne knew that he was going to enjoy shouting it out to the world.

So you think you can write?

It's your turn!

Mills & Boon® and Harlequin® have joined forces in a global search for new authors and now it's time for YOU to vote on the best stories.

It is our biggest contest ever—the prize is to be published by the world's leader in romance fiction.

And the most important judge of what makes a great new story?

YOU—our reader.

Read first chapters and story synopses for all our entries at
www.soyouthinkyoucanwrite.com

**Vote now at
www.soyouthinkyoucanwrite.com!**

HARLEQUIN®
entertain, enrich, inspire™

MILLS & BOON®

A sneaky peek at next month...

MODERN™

INTERNATIONAL AFFAIRS, SEDUCTION & PASSION GUARANTEED

My wish list for next month's titles...

In stores from 19th October 2012:

☐ A Night of No Return – Sarah Morgan

☐ Back in the Headlines – Sharon Kendrick

☐ Exquisite Revenge – Abby Green

☐ Surrendering All But Her Heart – Melanie Milburne

In stores from 2nd November 2012:

☐ A Tempestuous Temptation – Cathy Williams

☐ A Taste of the Untamed – Susan Stephens

☐ Beneath the Veil of Paradise – Kate Hewitt

☐ Innocent of His Claim – Janette Kenny

☐ The Price of Fame – Anne Oliver

Available at WHSmith, Tesco, Asda, Eason, Amazon and Apple

Just can't wait?

1012/01

Special Offers

Every month we put together collections and longer reads written by your favourite authors.

Here are some of next month's highlights— and don't miss our fabulous discount online!

On sale 19th October   On sale 2nd November   On sale 2nd November